Edinburgh Review 137

Haggis Hunting:

fifty years of new playwriting in Scotland

Edinburgh Review
Editor: Alan Gillis
Guest editors: Nicola McCartney and K.S. Morgan McKean
Assistant editor and production: Jennie Renton
Marketing and events: Lynsey May

The editors of this issue would like to thank all contributors, and also the following for their work on this edition: Alan Gillis, Jennie Renton, Rebecca McGann and Helen Davies of the Traverse Theatre, and Fiona Allen.

Advisory Board: Janice Galloway, Kathleen Jamie, Robert Alan Jamieson, James Loxley, Brian McCabe, Randall Stevenson, Alan Warner

Published by Edinburgh Review, 22a Buccleuch Place, Edinburgh EH8 9LN
edinburghreview@ed.ac.uk
www.edinburgh-review.com

Individual subscriptions (3 issues annually) £20 within the UK; £28 abroad. Institutional subscriptions (3 issues annually) £35 within the UK; £43 abroad. Most back issues are available at £7.99 each. You can subscribe online at www.edinburgh-review.com or send a cheque to Edinburgh Review, 22a Buccleuch Place, Edinburgh EH8 9LN

Edinburgh Review 137
Haggis Hunting: Fifty Years of New Playwriting in Scotland
ISBN 978-0-9564983-8-0
ISSN 0267-6672

Printed and bound in the UK
by Bell & Bain Ltd, Glasgow

Edinburgh Review
is supported by

ALBA | CHRUTHACHAIL

Contents

Poetry

This issue of *Edinburgh Review* is dedicated to
Gavin Wallace (1959–2013)

The sudden death of Gavin Wallace, with whom I edited *ER* in the '90s, shocked the literary community. I recall how his tiny, distinctively rune-like handwriting adorned the margins of scripts, marks of a scrutiny strictly attuned to perfect rhythm, a wily humour poised to seek sententiousness or nonsense, the keenest yet kindest eye, forgiving foibles, seeing promise. Latterly that fine intelligence helped nurture writers via his role at the Scottish Arts Council. His greatest achievement is the way that our community flourished with his support, and surely the best memorial is that this should continue, in his honour.

Robert Alan Jamieson

Foreword

This special edition celebrates two anniversaries: the fiftieth birthday of the Traverse Theatre, Scotland's home of new playwriting, and the fortieth of the Scottish Society of Playwrights. In association with these two cultural forces, the University of Edinburgh and the University of Greenwich will stage a conference in April 2013 entitled 'Haggis Hunting: Fifty Years of New Playwriting in Scotland'. Over the course of three days we will host a series of academic panels and a programme of performance events at the Traverse including play readings, debates and playwriting master classes, opening with a keynote address from leading Scottish theatre scholar Trish Reid. The second keynote address will be from the internationally renowned playwright David Greig, in which he wrestles with the problem of what it means to write a 'Scottish' play. A version of this speech – 'Hunting Kudu in Streatham' – is included in this publication.

The focus of Greig's article, of this edition and of much of the debate, is on language. How plays in Scotland are written and the ways in which they are written about. The inspiration for the title of our conference comes from Jan McDonald's 1979 essay: 'What is a Citizens' Theatre?', written in response to attacks against the theatre's Artistic Directors – Giles Havergal, Robert David MacDonald and Philip Prowse – and their European-influenced repertoire. Critics, including many Scottish playwrights who had not yet seen their work performed on that stage, dubbed the aesthetic 'a coterie theatre of esoteric high camp' and a 'house of illusion'[1] McDonald argued that Scottish theatre needed to be about something more than 'haggis hunting' for the next great Scottish play. In this edition of *Edinburgh Review*, we seek to contribute to and continue that debate. As we approach the Scottish Referendum on Independence in 2014, this conference asks that same question: what have we meant and what do we mean when we say a play is 'Scottish'? Written in Scots? About Scotland? Or simply made in Scotland?

The recent Theatre Sector Review, commissioned by Creative Scotland and undertaken by Christine Hamilton, concluded that 'new work is the lifeblood of Scottish theatre – often, although not always, this starts with the playwright', acknowledging the considerable international reach of that work. This edition includes seven extracts from unpublished work by leading Scottish playwrights. Please note that each playwright uses a different and personal style of punctuation in their work.

Nicola McCartney and K.S. Morgan McKean

1. Kershaw, Baz, (ed.), *The Cambridge History of British Theatre*, Vol. 3, Cambridge University Press (2004), P214.

David Greig

Hunting Kudu in Streatham

In 1987, Buff Hardie of 'Scotland the What' imagined the proprietor of the Ballater Toy Store receiving a call from Princess Diana on the occasion of Prince William's first Christmas in Balmoral.

Noo, fit wid he like for his Christmas, the loon?
…
Weel I'll tell ye fit I've got. It's something very suitable. It's oor ain special line in soft toys, and it is a cuddly futret.
…
A futret.
…
Div ye nae ken fit a futret is?
…
Futret. F-E-R-R-E-T, futret.
…
Noo fit size o' a futret wid ye like? We've got a dinkie futret, a mini futret, a life-size futret, a jumbo futret or a mega-futret.
…
Ye'd like a jumbo futret?
…
No, it disnae hae a trunk. No, it's got a string that ye pull, an' it sings Run, Rabbit, Run.
…
Weel, fit else div ye expect a futret tae sing?
…
Now is there onythin' else the loon wid like?
…

Fit aboot a rubber duke… for his bath?

…

A duke.

…

quack quack duke. Like Donald Duke. Donald Duke. He's a freen' o' Mickey Moose… Moose… M-O-U-S-E, Moose!

…

God, div ye nae understan' English, lassie?

In 1977, W.S. Graham, holed up by candlelight in his caravan near St Ives, sub-sisting on sheep's brains and scrounged greens, uttered a similarly anguished cry as he once more attempted to find the words to say just what he meant –

> O Language, you terrible surrounder
> Of everything.

I remember the moment I first faced the language question. It was 1990. I was living in the attic room of a shared house in Streatham Hill. It was the year Mrs Thatcher left office. I heard the news on my portable radio whilst walking down Streatham High Road and I did an involuntary leap into the air and side leg-kick – like Morecambe and Wise in *Bring Me Sunshine*. It was a brief moment of what felt like joy in what was otherwise a dull time.

Sometime around then, let's imagine it was that very evening, I sat in my attic at a primary school desk with a bottle of Bulgarian country wine at my elbow and looked out at the endlessness of Croydon. In front of me was either the beginning of a short story, or maybe it was a monologue? Or was it a fragment of dialogue? I wasn't sure. But whatever it was, it looked like writing.

Looking at it, I felt something stirring: less an emotion, more like a shifting of plates, a tidal tug pulling at all the atoms of my body, a feeling neither wholly explicable nor even desirable… a pull of the moon… I realised that I wanted to go home.

The only problem was, I didn't know where home was.

The thought process seemed to be this: If this is writing then perhaps I'm a writer. Writers have to come 'from' somewhere. So, if I want to write, I need to go back to the place where I'm from. But my relationship with 'from' is complicated.

My entire extended family, as far back as we've been able to go, come from the north east of Scotland. My mother's people are from Lossiemouth. My father's people are from Aberdeen. But not me, I was born in Edinburgh. I stayed there only briefly before my parents moved to Nigeria, where I grew up in a small tin-mining town. My father worked in the construction industry, creating Nigeria's post-colonial roads, parliaments, civil service offices – the concrete bones of a new country.

In Nigeria I attended an Italian nursery and then an American missionary school. My first dialect was Lombardy, my first accent Michigan Midwest. When I first arrived in Scotland, aged ten, I would ask my mother over and over again when we were going home. One year my parents took my brother and me north to a Hogmanay party in my Great Auntie Phyllis's house in Aberdeen. This was a proper working-class Hogmanay. There was a crowd in the front room, drink, smoke, and music. My great-uncle sang *Huntingtower* as a duet with his daughter. Another uncle did comic poems. Bothy ballads were sung. Everyone in the room was speaking to each other in the Doric. The room was full of heat and noise and smoke and it felt to me infused with a familiar unfamiliarity. My brother and I sat fixed on the sofa, neat in our Merchant Company school uniforms, shorts and blazer, silent and out of place.

Images from my memory are jumbled up with photographs of the time. Could the sofa have been orange? Why were we in school uniform? I remember big cylinders of John Player Special cigarettes on the coffee table in front of us. I remember the heavy, cushioned, bass sound of the cabinet record player and someone playing LPs by Kenneth McKellar and The Corries.

I wasn't speaking because I knew if I opened my mouth my half-American half-English vowels would come out and I'd get that particular look I knew, from aunties who studied me as if checking to see were I a changeling? A look which seemed to say, 'Are you sure he really belongs with us?'

The crowd in the front room stamped and clapped for another turn and someone gave a song, I don't remember which, but for a moment I was lost in it when suddenly a man I didn't recognise sat down beside me. Black suit and a glowing red face, cigarette in one hand, whisky tumbler in the other, he turned to me, leaned up close and said, 'I hope you're listening, son? *This is your heritage!*'

Ewan MacColl was the founding father of the folk revival, he was the man who first codified the policy that a singer should only sing material from their own country. Here's his partner, Peggy Seeger, writing about it:

> The policy was simple: If you were singing from the stage, you sang in a language that you could speak and understand. It didn't matter *what* you sang in the shower, at parties, while you were ironing or making love. But on stage in the Ballads and Blues Folk Club, you were a representative of a culture – you were interpreting a song that had been created within certain social and artistic parameters.

There's a scene I'm going to write one day, in which a young man comes home with his new university girlfriend to a working-class household in Aberdeen and starts telling his uncle all about where he's going wrong each Hogmanay singing that Calypso on the banjolele without reference to its social and artistic parameters. The play might build to a climax when his girlfriend, having learned from the Hogmanay party, goes to Cecil Sharp House and gives a dark, acapella rendering of *I'm the Quine Whit Dis the Strip at Inverurie*.

Recently I spoke to an anthropologist who made her life's work the study of the San or Bushmen people of the Kalahari. I talked to her because I'm interested in the way traditional hunter gatherer people tell stories. Humans evolved on the African savannah over a hundred millennia in small bands. At night, after they had eaten, and made a fire, and fucked… there must have still been an awful lot of night to fill and I wondered, what did they do? Did they tell each other stories?

Evolutionary biology can explain aspects of our nature. For example, why do humans, uniquely among the great apes, have no fur? Humans evolved for endurance hunting and lack of fur means we sweat and keep cool, whilst our mammalian prey, pursued over four hours of run walk run, will eventually keel over and die from heat exhaustion. Ancient hunting techniques are engraved in our very skin. Is it possible that ancient storytelling techniques are also somehow built into us?

How was the hunt today, Brian?

Not bad, Eric. Surprising moment with a Kudu.

Surprising, Brian?

Yes, I'd been chasing him for about four hours, run walk run, and suddenly, you know that place near big rock?

Big Rock Place, Brian?

That's right. There. He broke into the open. And then he turned, the Kudu, and he looked at me and… hang on – Sheila, you be the Kudu, I'll be me. Eric, would you mind being the rock?

So I asked the anthropologist how San people tell stories and she answered my question with a story of her own. She told me about her friend, a young man who had come to her asking if she knew how to make a traditional Bushman bow and arrow. She was bewildered.

'But, you are a Bushman? Surely you know how to make a traditional Bushman bow and arrow?'

'No,' the young man said. 'None of us know. None of us hunt anymore. The ones that do use guns. But I want to make a traditional San bow and arrow. I wondered,' he said, 'if some of you might know. Because you've studied us, haven't you? Maybe you could teach us?'

The anthropologist told me that shortly thereafter, an archaeology professor at a South African university had arranged workshops to teach young San men the traditional way to make bows and arrows. Her point was this – there is no traditional way the San people tell stories, unless they've learned it from an anthropologist.

So I raised my bow and arrow and I aimed… Sheila, that's it, eyes wider please… and the Kudu drew his hoof across the ground like this… can you do that for me, Sheila?

Can I snort, Brian?

Yes, you can snort.

[snort]

What about me?

You're just a rock, Eric, you stay still.

Ah right.

A young man in the Kalahari has to *choose* to be San. It's a decision he makes.

So he learns to make a bow. That night, in Streatham, I felt a tribal pull too. Could I write a Scottish play? Was there an anthropologist who'd teach me?

I once spent a summer translating Hugh MacDiarmid's poems from Lallans into English. Surely, David, you mean you spent a summer backpacking round Greece? No, I was a Scottish literature nerd. I had a subscription to *Cencrastus*, a Joy Hendry poster on my wall and back issues of *Chapman* stuffed in my jeans pocket. I used to skip school to go to the Poetry Library. I'd go down to the Water of Leith and sit by the river's stink reading Sidney Goodsir Smith and smoking roll-ups.

Lallans. It seems funny to think of it, now. MacDiarmid's attempt to invent a new old language for a new old country, but he meant it. He was quite fierce about it. In his own way as fierce as Ewan MacColl – '*It's yer heritage!*'

Robert Kemp's production of *Ane Pleasant Satyre of the Thrie Estatis* in 1948 laid the foundations of Lallans in the theatre. A piece of incontestably high art, written in unselfconscious Scots, it also, by the way, contains the first recorded use of the word 'cunt': and thus a golden thread of Scottish theatre is born, running all the way through to Gregory Burke. In 1960 Goodsir Smith's *The Wallace* was the first new old play in the old new tongue.

But by the seventies the Lallans project was running up against resistance. Historic epics, folk tales and academic comedies in synthetic Scots were seen as elite, esoteric concerns of little or no interest to ordinary folk. The working class of Scotland didn't speak Lallans. They spoke their Fife or Glaswegian or Doric. Writers and directors wanted to represent the reality of working-class life back to the people of Scotland and they saw that class was missing from MacDiarmid's picture. From this impulse a great stream of drama was produced which found high watermarks in the rediscovery of *Men Should Weep*, Joe Corrie's work, *The Bevellers*, *The Cheviot, the Stag* and others.

Unlike Brecht, whose working-class drama tried to shape the future, Scottish working-class drama was perhaps always already elegiac – a representation of something in the process of going. Men who had been miners now dressed up as miners to play the role of miners in mining museums. Men who had worked in the Clydeside shipyards now worked as ushers on Bill Bryden's production of *The Ship*. Just as the great roles of Scottish working-class drama were being first performed, the working class themselves were being done out of their roles in the real world.

Could a Scottish theatre be found which was forward-looking but which answered the class question? Was it possible to write for Scots but not in Scots? The answer was yes, and it came in an extraordinary burst of theatrical energy whose flame was lit by John Byrne.

From the first moment of the *Slab Boys'* verbal salvos it's clear that John Byrne doesn't write in Scots, but nor does he write in English either – he writes in pure John Byrne: an idiolect mixing high and low, Scots and English, poetic and prosaic – a non naturalistic, mongrel form that's individual but also, somehow, definingly tribal too. So *this* was what a Scottish play looked like! And John Byrne was only the first. In the 1980s Liz Lochead, Chris Hannan, Rona Munro, Iain Heggie, Peter Arnott and Jo Clifford all followed, each writing in heightened, poetic language of their own making. No insipid naturalism here – here were poetic idiolects which fizzed and popped and burst with the intense, crazy energy of writers who had realised that once you stopped writing in standard English, *anything* was possible – in *Animal* by Tom McGrath, a play staged at The Lyceum in 1978, most of the dialogue is written in animal grunts spoken by a pack of existential chimpanzees.

It turned out that Scottish theatre wasn't Scottish because it accurately represented the language of Scotland. It was Scottish because it PRODUCED the language of Scotland, remade it, re-imagined it anew.

And that is what I thought that night in Streatham, now onto my second bottle – pinched from my sleeping flatmate – I had half a monologue to finish, and finally I'd understood that I didn't have to write it in Lallans or Doric but I must fashion and find for it my own idiolect. Which in my case – *Europe, Stalinland, Petra* – was to be a language imagined to be in translation. Spoken in English but translated from the original Greig.

The next morning I put a note of apology and a bottle of Bull's Blood on the kitchen table and drove a hired van to Glasgow. Another in the long list of places I'm not quite from. My first plays were put on and I got to know David Harrower, Nicola McCartney, Steven Greenhorn, Mike Cullen, Zinnie Harris, Henry Adam, Ronan O'Donnell and other playwrights who were writing with the same released linguistic joy that I felt. The generation ahead of us had opened up a new country and we explored it, in fact we invented our own corners of the map.

I remember attending a performance of David Harrower's *Knives in Hens* at the Traverse in 1995. It was the post-show discussion that probably places it as the third or fourth ever performance of a play which was going to go on to be staged in virtually every theatre culture in the world but which was now only a Traverse 2 production of a Highland tour show. I loved the play. I was excited to hear the discussion. Would it be recognised? Would they get it? After the applause died down, David diffidently wandered out onto the stage and the first question came from a man at the back.

I enjoyed the play very much but I wonder, David, would you say it was 'A Scottish Play'?

And that was it. The discussion went on for what seemed like hours. Back and forth, back and forth. All the while David sat in silence. Next to him Martyn Bennett, who had made the music for the play, was silent too. Martyn was himself a bearer and breaker of traditions. I wonder what he thought. Probably he was glad he didn't deal in words.

After the discussion, I went to the gents. Next to me at the urinal stood Simon Donald. We stood in silence for a moment, reflecting, before Simon turned to me and said:

Two Scottish writers having a pish. But is it Scottish pish? That's the important question.

Sometimes when making a play, I've found it best to drive hard towards what I perceive to be the biggest problem because, when embraced, a problem can turn out to be its own solution. The Scottish Renaissance began because Scottish writers felt peripheral. MacDiarmid wanted to give Scotland back its centrality. He wasn't able to do that but his failure resulted in something else, something better: a fragmented theatre in which authors embraced their peripherality and set themselves at the centre of their own worlds. Now, in the 21st century, the embrace of the margins is mainstream. The old accoutrements of a nation state – a language, a canon, and a four-walled national theatre – those forms of national identity seem outmoded. Too, too solid, like a prison. I wonder if, in missing out on them, we didn't have a lucky escape.

Here on the periphery I make direct connections with theatres in Spain, Norway, Germany, Japan and the Middle East. I'm able to make those connections partly because people there feel themselves also to be peripheral. Feeling peripheral is mainstream. Feeling oneself to be mainstream – that's a marginal position.

Forced to wait till 2005, we leapfrogged the Doric pillars and pediments of four-walled national theatres and instead brought into being a National

Theatre without walls which has become a means by which our theatre makers can reflect back to the people of Scotland an image of themselves unlimited by form, language or, indeed, heritage.

Recently I was speaking to another anthropologist. (I hunt anthropologists with the same persistence our ancestors hunted Kudu.) This anthropologist told me that people in traditional societies usually speak many languages. Each individual language is spoken by a very small number of speakers, often only numbering in the hundreds. Usually there is a taboo against marrying within one's own language group, so – inevitably – it's common that a person's father and mother come from different language groups. When one considers that in any tribe there would also be a number of couples each of whom would speak different languages and each of whom would provide the children of the tribe with care, one can see that in a traditional society a child would be being brought up amongst a babble of words in a streams of diverse languages. Data from Amazonia and Papua New Guinea suggest that the number of languages a person in a traditional society might expect to speak fluently is somewhere between five and fifteen.

It is in our DNA to feel at home when we are surrounded by different languages.

Sheila?

Yes, Brian?

Can you sing the Kudu death song for us?

Which one do you mean, Brian?

The version you do, in your language, Sheila.

Oh, right. No worries, Brian – I'll give that a go.

Oh, I like that song!

Quiet Eric, you're a rock.

Sorry.

Alasdair Gray has said that a city doesn't really exist until it's been written about. In saying that, he identified a space which exists in parallel with the concrete world, a space of the imagination. W.S. Graham called it

'The Constructed Space' – opened up by art, in which we locate ourselves imaginatively. Art doesn't just map that space, it physically conjures it. The more art that is available to us, the larger the imaginative space available for us to inhabit. The more space we inhabit, the more we can locate ourselves. The more we can locate ourselves, the easier it is to navigate, to find our way out of ourselves and towards new possibilities.

Countries need infrastructure – the secretariats and parliament buildings and roads my father built in Nigeria in the 1970s, for example. But art provides a second, invisible infrastructure by which another country, a country of the imagination, is forged. Every time we ensure there is money to fund the staging of a play, or a gig, every bursary we give a writer, every book of poetry whose publication we subsidise, we nurture our nation's invisible infrastructure. The value gained from those small amounts spent on art is permanent, not temporary, and it is carried as a private gift by the individual citizens who encounter the art. It is very good value for money.

Recently Sidse Knudsen, the star of the Danish TV series *Borgen*, came to the Filmhouse in Edinburgh. In *Borgen* she plays the female prime minister of a small northern country. She enacts this imaginary woman's life with care and detail. The Filmhouse was packed. Hundreds of fans came to watch a special screening and meet their heroine. Chief among the fans was deputy first minister, Nicola Sturgeon. She interviewed Sidse Knudsen from the stage.

'Why do we like *Borgen*?' Ms Sturgeon asked the audience. 'Maybe it gives us a glimpse of the country we could be.'

When, in the imaginative world, we encounter versions of ourselves we are given a jolt of pure energy and possibilities open up. By showing us who we are, drama also shows us who we could be.

So what happened with the Kudu, Brian?

Oh, right, yes, well, I looked the poor beast in the eye –
It dragged its hoof across the ground
It shook
And then it said – Sheila?

Yes?

Kudu death song?

Oh… ok…

This is me being the Kudu:
[She sings]
Surely there must be something to say,
Maybe not suitable but at least happy
In a sense here between us two whoever
we are? Anyhow here we are and never
Before have we two faced each other who face
Each other now across this abstract scene
Stretching between us. This is a public place
Achieved against subjective odds and then
Mainly an obstacle to what I mean.

It is like that, remember. It is like that
Very often at the beginning till we are met
By some intention risen up out of nothing.
And even then we know what we are saying
Only when it is fixed and dead.
Or maybe, surely, of course we never know
What we have said, what lonely meanings are read
Into the space we make. And yet I say
This silence here for in it, I might hear you.

And saying that the poor beast died. Just keeled over. Odd it was, strange. I didn't even get to fire my arrow from my traditionally made bow.

Very beautiful death scene there, Sheila. Gorgeous.

Thanks, Eric.

That song you gave us at the end, Sheila, was that 'The Constructed Space' by W.S. Graham?

It was, Eric.

Thanks for that, Sheila. It was lovely.

You're welcome.

Now, has anyone else got a good story?

JL Williams

Time Breaks the Heart

Her watch is posted from the south.
Its black box ticks the whole way.

The accident happens, the funeral.
The flowers fade.

Grain in silos shifts with powdery sighs.
Light drifts, changes.

Her smell is gone. The voice of the beloved,
like any old memory, strays.

Her watch, in its dark drawer,
stops at a quarter to eight.

A gale blows loose a bird's nest
lined with silken gold-red strands,

and when I find it in the wind-wrecked yard
I see her, again – at the window, brushing her hair.

The Words for Longing

even in Kyoto,
hearing a cuckoo,
I long for Kyoto
                    —Basho

1

This spring the jasmine
winds its tendrils joyously
around water pipes.

I've watched it grow,
leaf and flower and yellow,
sleep and grow.

A baby reaches
for a beam of sun,
closes her empty hand.

Her hair of white smoke, her lips
fragile as jasmine blossoms
on the cusp of dawn.

2

A doctor tells the story of a cruel dementia
that robbed a poor woman
of nearly all her language.

When her husband died
the doctor reported concern
that she would not have the words to grieve.

He asked her how she felt,
was moved to tears by her reply;

'I am in a place,
and it is only me
and the place.'

3

You wake in my arms.
There is no air between us.
Still, I reach for you.

La Dolce

What rhymes with time?
That lime on the lime tree's branch, death.

It seems so simple in Italian, rhyming.
Breath between lips that dimples cheeks.

The whistle coquettish and low.
To know him, once, twice, to feed him a drink

Flavoured with the fruit of the lime tree's branch.
Its sweet zing, the tolling of the golden wall

Tapped by the fingers of the blithe boy.
His life a sweet-tart fruit to be mined for its juice.

Gondolas midst the ombra weave
As he lies singing in the arms of love.

And he grows old now, though he knows it not…
his voice becoming sublime.

Pool Hall School

Of a boy who shot his brother
and walked away.
Of a way to watch a death
and feel it's pleasing,
framed in a metal square and pressed beneath glass.
This much we've learned.

Of a quiet mascara-friendly reserve
that reveals no more in mourning
than the token rain.

Of a veil of black lace
draping whatever thin shadows
topple through grey light
over our faces like bars.

How to lose and let go
of the loved one, not the self
and spend the afternoon after the funeral
pacing a pool hall,
beer in hand upon hand,
lit by screens alive
with massacres wrenching by
in the pot-holed streets.

This much we've learned –
how to hit with cold precision
one shiny ball against another
so it reflects in garish distortion
bloody eyeless faces bending toward a speechless hole.

Jo Clifford

Extract from *Sex, Chips and the Holy Ghost*

Production Credits

This play was first performed at Òran Mór on 30 Jan 2012 as part of the A Play, a Pie, and a Pint season.

Cast:
HE   David Walshe
SHE   Jo Clifford.
Director: Susan Worsfold

The play is set in Òran Mór.
David MacLennan has just made his announcement, and left.
Enter HE and SHE.
HE is a priest, SHE a transsexual nun. He pushes on an executive wheelie. She carries a bulging carpet bag.

HE   Excuse me!

SHE   Mr Maclemon!

HE   Too late.

SHE   You tell them.

HE   Ladies and gentlemen,

Ignore what that man just said.
You'll not be seeing that 'Sex Chips and the Holy Ghost'.

SHE   Not today. Not ever.

HE   There'll be no play.

SHE   It's been cancelled.

HE   Erased from the record.

SHE   Wiped off the face of the earth.

BOTH Thank God.

HE   There'll be no Jo Clifford.

SHE   And particularly no David Walshe.

SHE   That wicked wicked pair.

HE   They have been placed in a holy house of correction.

SHE   Where they will receive their just measure of repentance.

HE   So. We repeat:

BOTH You will not be seeing a play.

HE   You will be witnessing the struggle between good and evil.

SHE   The struggle between light and dark.

HE   The drama of real life. House lights, please.

SHE   Evil thrives in darkness.

HE   House lights, please.

SHE   House lights this minute.

House lights come on.

HE   Good for you, Sister.

They see the audience.

HE & SHE   Oh Jesus.

SHE   Heaven help us all. The suffering.

HE   The wasted potential.

SHE   The poor lost souls.

HE   Given over to the powers of darkness

SHE   Helplessly enslaved to the sins of the flesh.

HE   Not to mention the hours and hours of lost productivity.

SHE   Thank God we are able to help.

HE   Ladies and gentlemen, let me explain. Following a transparent and highly competitive tendering process we have won the contract to cleanse these premises of the evil influences that currently infest it.

SHE   Holy and much needed work.

HE   We at Soul Clean dot com guarantee to rid your home or place of work of any negative vibrations that inhibit growth, stunt productivity and diminish the potential of wealth creation. What you are about to witness, ladies and gentlemen, is a highly scientific process that has been researched for millennia.

SHE   It draws on mystic traditions from the East. That St Francis Xavier brought back from Japan. St Francis Xavier, ladies and gentlemen, just in case you have forgotten, is one of the founders of the Jesuits.

HE   And the Jesuits are the richest religious order of them all.

SHE   St Francis gave knowledge of the Christian faith to the East and the East gave us the secret knowledge in return. The esoteric knowledge that underpins the economy of Hong Kong.

HE   And I need hardly tell you, ladies and gentlemen, that Hong Kong is the economic powerhouse of the world. And the Vatican is one of the richest states in the world. Their investments underpin the entire banking system.

SHE   This is at the heart of our work.

HE   We hold the exclusive franchise.

SHE   This is what we told dear Mr Beattie, the owner of this establishment.

HE   And this is how we gained the contract.

SHE   This is a perfectly safe procedure, ladies and gentlemen, and provided you follow instructions, you will come to no actual physical harm. But if you do not, God have mercy on your soul.

HE   iPad, Sister.

SHE   iPad, Father.
Using the latest modern technology we first of all establish the physical dimensions of the site in order to estimate the strength of spiritual signal required.

HE   And draw up the invoice. Length.

SHE   Having calculated the physical dimensions…

HE   Width. Height.

SHE   The Father will then factor in the PEF of the customer mass.

HE   Physical dimensions established. Now for the spiritual dimension.

SHE   PEF is the Prone to Evil Factor which we measure according to guidelines laid down by the millennial wisdoms of the Catholic Church. Certain worldly practices followed by certain worldly individuals among you leave you particularly open to evil influence.

HE   Freemasons?

SHE   Any Freemasons?

[pause]

SHE   Oh ladies and gentlemen, I am very disappointed in you.
Please don't be ashamed.
Of course we understand the Masons are supposed to be a secret organisation, but this really is no excuse.

HE   You are transparent to the all-seeing eye of God. And the Sister's psychic nose.

SHE   I smell twenty. God forgive them.

HE   Cecil Rhodes scholars?

[pause]

SHE   Father, I know these so-called scholars are on the Vatican's list.

Along with Amaranths and Rotarians. But I sense we may have more habitual sinners among us. Bankers for instance.

HE   Sister, no one is going to admit to being a banker.

SHE   Then more vulnerable victims of Satan's evil wiles. Yoga practitioners.

HE   People who meditate.

SHE   New age hippies. Using crystals.

HE   Playing Dungeons and Dragons.

SHE   Wicca.

HE   Shriners. Satanic music lovers.

SHE   The Father means heavy metal fans.

HE   Followers of the occult.

SHE   The father means economists. I also sense there are many many people here who masturbate.

HE   And read romantic novels. Masturbate, read romantic novels. And are practising homosexuals.

SHE   People using contraception.

HE   Having sex outside marriage.

SHE   Having abortions.

HE   Having suicidal thoughts.

SHE   Attempting suicide.

[pause]

SHE   You may think, ladies and gentlemen, we're making this up.

HE   You couldn't make this up.

SHE   This is the official list.

HE   Www.T-R-O-S-C-H dot org.

SHE   Forward slash church.

HE   Dot html.

SHE   And shortly we will be doing what we can to cleanse this poisonous atmosphere with the prayer created by his Holiness Pope Leo the thirteenth.

HE   It's certainly needed, Sister. I strongly suspect this room is full of people eating pies.

SHE   Surely not.

HE   And drinking pints.

SHE   It's just too appalling to contemplate.

HE   It is the West End.

SHE   Father, that's no excuse.
           This place is a den of iniquity.

HE   This is a big contract.

SHE   This is a big contract.
           We'll need at least a gallon of the very best, and very coldest, water

of Lourdes.

HE I'll put it in the invoice. I'll send it this minute.

SHE No time like the present, Father.

HE Physical dimensions plus prone to evil factor times one hundred and eighty-two plus extra holy water plus labour costs plus VAT. Send.

SHE Isn't technology amazing?

HE Spirit meter.

SHE Spirit meter, Father.
The Father is now preparing his high tech equipment.
Which we use to pinpoint spots in particular need of cleansing.
Which I douse with the holy water.
This water is guaranteed 100% holy and will not stain your clothes.
It will, however, remove the stains on your souls.

HE Activate. Intensity rising.

He turns on his machine and dashes off to a corner.

HE Spots of high density over here, Sister.

SHE Coming.

HE Critical in this corner.

SHE Coming!

HE Her.

SHE Yes, Father.

HE   Him.

SHE   Yes, Father.

HE   Them.

SHE   All of them?

HE   Every single one.

SHE   Yes, Father.

HE   Emergency!!

SHE   Coming!

HE   It's upstairs.

SHE   Upstairs!

HE   What's upstairs?

SHE   I think it's a bar.

HE   That would explain it. And to think this was once a holy house of God.

SHE   Shocking.

Both sigh.

HE   Still. With God's help, I think for now we have accomplished all we can. Tissue, Sister.

SHE   Tissue, Father.

HE   Thank you, Sister. Smudge me.

SHE   Smudge, Father. Ladies and gentlemen, We smudge with the highest quality sage. 100% organic.

You'll note that the principles behind our work are highly scientific and tested in the Vatican laboratories.

The Father has just withdrawn into himself in preparation for the prayers.

With these prayers we invoke the positive energies of the blessed saints to complete the cleansing process. And then we corral the negative vibrations in a circle of salt… Salt of the oceans.

Fruits of the earth and fruits of the sea.

And are you ready, ladies and gentlemen. Ladies and gentlemen and transsexuals? Are you ready? Are you prepared? We need your consent: the freely given consent of our customers. Otherwise all the labour which we are carrying out at a considerable personal risk to ourselves, will be in vain

You see, the Devil's greatest achievement here in this gathering is to convince you that he does not exist.

But he does exist, here and now, and he is at work.

The Devil wants our unhappiness, the Devil wants to drive us from our true selves. The Devil wants us to strive to become rich over and above every other consideration. The Devil wants us to trample on our brothers and sisters as we scramble to reach the top of the tree. The Devil wants you to stay in the job you detest, to stay with the partner that oppresses and cheats you. The Devil wants you to be tied down by your guilt, your fear and your shame. The Devil will do everything he can to drive us from our true and liberated selves.

But we at Soul Clean dot com are here to overcome the Devil's work. How fortunate we are, ladies and gentlemen and transsexuals, to be in such safe hands.

For the Father is the Master of Prayer.

Note his utter absorption. His total stillness. You may see a beam of light coming down from the heavens, perhaps containing a white dove. Don't be alarmed. This is perfectly normal.

You may see a pillar of flame, burning bush, a supernatural being with dazzling white wings.

Don't be alarmed. This is perfectly normal.

You may hear a voice 'This is my beloved child in whom I am well pleased'. And you will know it is true. Because, ladies and gentlemen and transsexuals, whoever we are, the spirit is pleased with us. The Lord saw us all in our mother's womb and formed us to be the people we are and called us by our true name and blessed us. The Father is now communing directly with the saints.

Let us be silent for a moment.

[pause]

HE   We invoke St Edward, once King of England, murdered by his nobles because of his passion for his lover, Piers. Whose virtue was denied, but whose sainthood was revered by his people.

SHE   Pray for us.

HE   We invoke St Matthew who like us was an outcast.

SHE   Pray for us.

HE   We invoke St Philip who baptised the eunuch.

SHE   Pray for us.

HE   We invoke St Sebastian for his beautiful naked body.

SHE   Pray for us.

HE   We invoke St Anthony because he preached to the fishes and is the saint of lost causes.

SHE   Pray for us.

HE   St Julian because she prayed to God the Mother.

SHE   Pray for us.

HE   St Uncumber because in order to avoid marrying a man she detested she grew a long black bushy beard.

SHE   Pray for us.

HE   And we invoke St John of the Cross because he loved everyone.

SHE   Pray for us.

HE   And because he utterly identified herself as the Bride of Christ.

SHE   Pray for us.

HE   St Sergius and St Bacchus because they were lovers and because their tormentors dressed them in women's clothes to humiliate them.

SHE   But who instead gloried in their women's gowns.

HE   Pray for us. Have mercy on us all.

SHE   Let all unhappiness be driven from this place
in the name of all these saints and rebels
drive unhappiness from this place.
And may everyone here become connected with their true loving selves.

HE & SHE   Amen amen amen amen.

K.S. Morgan McKean

Something (Un)Spoken

In his 2011 Keynote Presentation to the Theatre and Performance Research Association conference, Ian Brown surveyed the history of Scottish theatre and looked at the different languages and dialects representing Scottish voices on the stage.[1] In his conclusion, he anticipated that in addition to Scots and Gaelic, future Scottish voices to be staged might include dialogue written in Urdu. Currently, companies such as Ankur Productions[2] mentor young writers of different ethnicities, as do the Playwrights' Studio, Scotland, who also had Tanika Gupta as an Associate Playwright in 2008 to 2009. The voices of Scots from different ethnic backgrounds are to be heard on stages in Scotland – in plays such as *Pandas*, Rona Munro's 2011 play for the Traverse – but they are predominantly written by white writers for a predominantly white audience. Two plays by two of Scotland's leading playwrights, both on stage in 2011, create Scottish Muslim characters through different uses of silence, thus recording an absence as well as a presence in how they articulate and represent 'other' Scottish voices.[3] In *Yellow Moon* by David Greig and *A Slow Air* by David Harrower, there is present an articulation of 'other' Scottish voices that is not just an acknowledgement of, but an engagement with the idea of absence, of silence, in the representation of 'cultural difference'[4] in Scotland and on the Scottish stage.[5]

Joyce McMillan describes *A Slow Air* as 'so profound in its local sense of place, so global in its reach and its humanity [that it] will leave your sense of the country we live in subtly shaken and changed, for good'.[6] *A Slow Air* is comprised of monologues spoken by Morna and her estranged brother Athol. Athol's world is changed 'for good', his Houston community brought together and thus in a sense defined by the 2007 Glasgow airport attack, fusing 'out of the ashes'.[7] This event ends distance within the locality and in another way – between Athol and his wife – he doesn't continue his affair in Glasgow that day or any other (pp. 43–44). The day of the attack marks a point when neighbours established new bonds and began to 'look out for each other'. A day that brought a sense of belonging for Athol, previously perceiving himself viewed as 'other' in Houston: 'maybe they've smelt Edinburgh on me' (p. 7).

This remark, made by Athol to his wife in the play's opening monologue, engages with the idea of difference present in the narrative throughout. Morna, when finally reunited with Athol by her son, Joshua, teases her brother about the 'Weegie' inflections in his voice, and Athol comments on the Edinburgh in Josh's speech. The differences are apparent on the page as well as the stage, with Morna's use of Scots more prevalent than Athol's. Joshua has told Athol about Morna's illness, something she dismisses as not serious (p. 37), though her son draws himself with an urn awaiting her ashes. Even when the siblings meet, some of their communication is silent: 'I was watching Morna, her eyes fixed on Josh and Rachel [Josh's girlfriend]. She looks at me. I look at her. She smiles. I see the pain and the fear. And I know. And she knows.' Of course for much of the play, Morna and Athol literally communicate through their silence, their history spoken to the audience, though much of it shared.

The past is a present country in *A Slow Air*. And similarity as well as difference is there. One of Joshua's illustrations recalls the family history that Morna recounts when challenging her younger self with her own tiny place in the world:

> Aw the family that came before me. Drivin buses, cuttin hair, pullin pints, polishin silver. Hard lives in black an white. Wi nae other choice. I see that now.
>
> My grandmother's mother worked in the fields, for God's sake. Howkin tatties out near Dalkeith. Fuckin gettin up in the mornin tae stand at a hirin fair, her name called out by a factor. My grandfather who fought in the Second World War. [...] He saw the Luftwaffe flyin up the Forth. Heard the drone o them, up above him in the sky. I mean, who the fuck am I? (p. 14).

The image of the Luftwaffe in the sky resonates with the image of the aeroplane trail lingering in 'the slow air' Athol sees on his walk with Josh (he can't bring himself to call him Joshua, after the U2 album). Josh asks to see Athol's family photographs, revealing an absence in his nephew's narrative of who he is in the sense of where he comes from in 'pictures he'd never seen'. Revealing also a family tradition of jumping in photos – initiated by Athol's father, usually turning from fun to frustration through failure. The sense of continuity across the generations comes again at the end of the play when, on different station platforms, Joshua holds up his phone and instructs his mother and uncle to jump (p. 45).

McMillan describes the 'disturbing panorama' in the play 'of ordinary life in Scotland's Central Belt today; from the universal western effort to maintain a comfortable middle-class way of life in a new age of terror, to the divisions of class and income that corrode our society, the strands of culture and music that still sometimes unite it, and the strange persistence of the seemingly fragile bonds of family'. The count at the end up to the jump that unites Morna and Athol, connects not only with their father's onerous demands but another event recalled by Athol in the play's history. When Joshua visits his uncle's home in Houston, it is with an awareness of where the terrorists who attacked Glasgow airport lived. They break into the empty house, Athol vomits and his nephew again takes photographs on a phone and intones the command to Athol to 'jump'. Athol attempts to erase the episode as he removes the photos of '[t]hat dead, empty house' from his phone, this action accentuating rather than eradicating a tension that exists throughout the play: 'I pressed delete. Delete. Delete' (p. 45).

Joshua himself first presents as an absence, leaving his note ('*I was here today*') unsigned, his explanation for anonymity revealing the difference in the way the two men see the world:

Some Asian guy over there was watching me, he said.
Aye, my neighbour.
He shrugged. (p. 12)

The knowledge Joshua displays of the terrorists through the questions he asks his uncle, reveals his obsession with the case. The detail that he doesn't know is the part his uncle played in the story: '*I'm to blame*' Athol tells him,

'*It was all my fault*' (p. 18). As a contractor sharing small talk with a potential client, Athol disclosed airport security information to Kafeel Ahmed, who set himself on fire during the failed attack. Joshua ridicules the '*Crap terrorists*', but Athol is haunted by the image of his unsuspecting self: 'Did they laugh at me? Pity me? Letting me into their house to show their normality. A man who put on a shirt and tie and rang their doorbell, samples under his arm. No idea. Pathetic fucking stupid fucking'. The sentence ends without a stop, punctuated in the recollection by the image of him back in the empty house, throwing up. Joshua explores the house, mocking the dead former occupant: '*Hey, Kafeel, you stupid burnt bastard, did you make it to heaven? Did you get your seventy-two virgins?*' (p. 31). His taunts resonate with the illustrations Morna finds: 'There was some cartoon character called Crap Terrorist. Then loads o pages o naked girls wi numbered signs round their necks' (p. 33). Joshua shows Athol other drawings he has done of real and imagined images of events surrounding the attack, his uncle again unable to fully articulate the discomfort he feels ('[…] people were still' p. 23). Joshua finds it hard to realise the image of the bombers he holds, one that 'others' and dehumanises them entirely:

> *That doctor worked in the hospital in Paisley for a whole year,* I says. *Went to work every day and made people better.*
>   *Must've really hated his job,* Josh said. (p. 29).

The exchange, like the play, explores the complexities that Joshua denies.

Joshua's contempt extends beyond the bombers, saying '*trust Scotland to produce such crap terrorists*'. Whilst the statement simultaneously takes in and 'others' the bombers, it is clear throughout the play that Joshua's racism is all-encompassing in relation to South Asian Scots. Athol has a shared joke with his neighbours, the Rabbanis, about their daughter's fear of his dog. In their hearing, Joshua surmises that '*Asians are scared of dogs* […] *They think they're unclean*'. The issue is problematic – Joshua makes statements that reveal the essentialism present in his thinking, but in this case it is borne out within the play, as Mr Rabbani later tells Athol '*It is dirty*' (p. 32). Athol retrieves his dog from the cowering Rabbani's home, reaching for the lead that isn't there, indicating that the escape has been facilitated, if not orchestrated, by Joshua. Earlier in the play we learn of Athol's instruction to always keep Clay on the lead, as he has a habit of jumping up on people, scaring them (p. 17). Joshua refuses to engage with Athol's attempt to confront him and the issue becomes another silence unspoken within the play.

Joshua, as the only representative of his generation, has an idea of community that is less inclusive than his uncle's. Less inclusive than the figures his mother invokes as she recalls 'marchin tae the Meadows' in '"92':

> Hamish leadin us in 'Freedom Come All Ye'. Campbell Christie's big red fitba o a face. An aw, Willie McIlvanney, boomin intae his mike, *We're all mongrels in this nation.*
>
> I was near the front. *Who're you calling a mongrel?*, I shouted, *I'm a pure bred bitch.* (p. 19).[8]

In the course of this monologue, Morna reveals the different positions she has held in relation to inclusivity, her memories encompassing prejudice against English students whilst 'rabid SNP' (though one of her arguments with her brother was over her unpatriotic taste in rock music)[9] and the hopes for a diversity and equality found in Henderson's Scots-language anti-imperialist song and McIlvanney's politics. Her stories reveal also the class and sectarian divisions that are also marks of difference in Scotland, the former of particular concern to Harrower who argues that '[e]quality of opportunity is dead in Britain'. Alex Salmond is among those who have drawn on McIlvanney's words to support his vision for the nation:

> There will be no cricket tests in a free Scotland. We see diversity as a strength not a weakness of Scotland and our ambition is to see the cause of Scotland argued with English, French, Irish, Indian, Pakistani, Chinese and every other accent in the rich tapestry of what we should be proud to call, in the words of Willie McIlvanney 'the mongrel nation' of Scotland.[10]

There's a sense in which Harrower uses silence to show that we don't quite have the words to explain the complexities, the subtleties. That both personally and politically our own histories are complex and dense and painful and our present so often disappointing. He describes the difference (and distance) between the characters: 'One's a bit of a f***-up and one's done pretty well for themselves. It's about where do they think they are now, where are they in Scotland, where is Scotland in the modern world?'. The form of *A Slow Air* exposes the space between the characters, each one providing an illustration of the space within – pains unvoiced, secrets not shared. There are moments that can be described as occurring in the same liminal space in comics that Joshua has tried to describe to Morna: 'He keeps tryin tae explain to me about the gutter. That's what they call the white space between the boxes o a comic. Where the artist decides what happens next. What tae draw in the next box. Anythin can happen in the gutter, he said.' (p. 15). First performed by real-life brother and sister Lewis and Kathryn Howden, the sense of connection between the characters extended further in the original production, an overlapping of boundaries, a blurring. The title of the play appears in one of the final scenes described in the play, when a musician – previously heckled by Morna – joins the family table and sings. It is recalled by Athol's description of seeing only a trail of a plane's flight path: 'There was the faint rumble of a plane we couldn't see, just the ribbon of its vapour trail fading above us in the slow air'. Just a trace. Something lingering. Something lost.[11]

David Greig's title also has the trace of a song in it, *Yellow Moon: The Ballad of Leila and Lee*. Silent Leila and Stag Lee go on the run into the Highlands after Lee stabs his mother's boyfriend. The play was commissioned by TAG Theatre Company and toured schools, but has been revived and toured extensively to both youth and adult audiences. The play has five characters and, in the original production (and in the development period) was performed by four actors. Much of the dialogue is third person narration of a character's internal thoughts voiced (in the original production) by another actor. At times the actors behave as a collective, a chorus ('Did we mention Lee's mum's boyfriend?'),[12] and in places the narration shifts tenses, telling one version of events (early on we hear Leila give extensive answers to Lee's questions) before revealing the reality (Leila answers the same questions with silence): 'Of course she didn't really say that. / She didn't really say any of that.' (p. 22). The ballad points to the parts of the story that are incomplete ('let's skip ahead') and at times recreates memory's jumbled structure: fragments and images without words. In one of these moments, in Scene 15, the narration is voiced in the first person – it is not necessarily Leila speaking, but it is with her voice: 'I don't have a story for that last week.' (p. 45). Thus do we as an audience learn of the characters' histories, fears and desires which prompt their often monosyllabic answers and failures of communication with one another, thus does Greig sound the silence.

The form is closely connected to Silent Leila, since both character name and form were inspired by the same source:

> The seeds of Silent Leila came from a young woman I met when […] [s]he was part of a workshop I was giving […] in Palestine […]The girl wrote interestingly but […] I didn't particularly notice her. Then one day over lunch in the big empty hotel […] I heard laughter. I wandered over to its source and I found that this girl was holding court to all the other students and telling what appeared to be an hilarious story. The table […] was convulsed with laughter. She held them with all the skill of a stand up comedian [...]
>
> My colleague […] said that the girl had recently lost her father, not long before that her brother, then her mother all in relatively quick succession. […] On the death of her father, she had fallen into a kind of shock and had stopped speaking. Her relatives hatched different plans to make her speak: her uncle 'was driving her to school one morning when suddenly he slammed on the brakes and screamed. The girl was so surprised that she shouted out something like 'what the fuck was that!' And after that she had no problems speaking again. And now, she said, you could hardly ever get her to shut up.
>
> I was interested, thereafter, in the way that silence is often not the result of having nothing to say but of having too much to say – so much that it forms a kind of paralysis, a blockage.
>
> So the internal monologue of a silent person became a mode I wanted to play around with.[13]

Yellow Moon's Leila gives the following explanation for her silence (except she doesn't, of course):

LEE　　　How come you don't say much, Silent Leila?
　　　　　How come you don't speak?

LEILA　　I don't speak because most people aren't worth speaking
　　　　　to.

LEE   Did you always not speak or did you just stop one day?

LEILA   I stopped one day. I was sitting on the wall at school and Mr Hopeton passed me and he said, 'Everything all right, Leila?' And I looked at him, and he said it again: 'Everything all right?' And he smiled at me and I like Mr Hopeton so I thought, 'I don't know, is everything all right?' It seemed such a complicated question. I didn't know. I didn't answer and eventually he just said, 'Oh well. Good good.' And I realised – people hear what they want to hear, it doesn't matter what you say. So I just decided to stop. I stopped bothering. [...]
It's just easier. (p. 22)

The silence leaves space onto which others speculate about or project their ideas about Leila:

Most people just assume she's quiet because she's Muslim.

The way she dresses is Muslim, isn't it?

Maybe Muslim girls aren't allowed to speak.

Maybe she can't speak English.

Most people don't worry about it.

It's not as if we particularly want to ask her anything, is it? (p. 5)

The narrators are short on specifics in terms of Leila's background – we only learn that they think her professional parents arrived as refugees 'from some sort of war' in the 1990s who now live in an affluent area. We know that she has visited the Great Mosque in Damascus and that it was there, at twelve, that she heard God speak to her and tell her 'she was special in the manner of one day perhaps saving the world' (p. 10). In terms of her Muslim identity, however, it is through the narrators rather than Leila that she is identified. Of course her name implies it – Leila Suleiman is a Middle Eastern Muslim name – but it's religion rather than ethnicity that the narrators use to 'other' her, though religion doesn't feature beyond this. There are a number of choices being made. Perhaps a number of ways in which one – with prejudgement that characterises Muslim experience as South Asian Muslim experience – might expect to hear the silence broken differently. 'Remember', writes Greig, 'the Islamic-ness of the daughter of two middle-class, left wing Palestinian refugees who've lived in Scotland since the seventies (my imaginary background for Leila) is not necessarily the same as the Islamic-ness of a family of Pakistani origin living in Glasgow'.

So there is no halal diet for Leila, no sense of shame or loss of *izzat* in relation to female sexuality, and no expectation for her to follow her parents into medical professions, but instead a challenge to such essentialist presumptions that can dominate Western attitudes to Muslim women. Of course it's possible that the interpretation of Leila's characterisation may depend on the ethnicity of the actor playing the role. In the original production she was played by an actor with a Hindu name (Nalini Chetty)[14] having been workshopped in the development process by a white British actor (Kirsten Hazel Smith). The decision to make Leila both non-white and Muslim appears then to be a deliberate one by the playwright and/or director, but this is not in fact the case. There is a sense in which difference is written into the character and then it is not. That there is articulation and then silence. This can then be interpreted as either a challenge to essentialism or – after August Wilson – an act of assimilation, creating ground on which to stand where there is none.[15] There is nothing in the play to dictate the ethnicity of the performer or the character, however, and Greig suggests that 'she could be a secular white girl from Bosnia and the whole story would still make sense'.

Greig's inspiration for Leila came from a number of sources in addition to the Palestinian Leila he met at the end of the 1990s: Asian friends from school and Scottish Asian children at school with his who he describes as '[m]iddle class kids in small towns in Scotland'. Although the magazines Leila reads are full of white Western women, her media obsession is one that Greig sees replicated in 'Syria, Egypt, Palestine, Tunisia etc' where young women 'watched Beiruti pop stars on tv, they read gossip magazines, they wondered about their futures, they flirted with boys' and 'were not so different to [...] young women in workshops in Kirkcaldy and Inverkeithing'. Greig 'never felt he was being untrue to Leila's background' and perhaps – given the ambiguity in the text as to what this background is – the character can be viewed as a transcultural figure, whose hybridity is interchangeable and her personal story again reflected in the play's form. This form is liminal, frequently an articulation of an 'in-between' space for characters and action, moving between the sensate and subliminal, reality and imagination, speech and silence. Leila articulates an internal division in the play:

> If we could hear the thoughts inside Leila's head we'd hear this:
>
> This hand doesn't belong to me.
> This arm doesn't belong to me.
> I'm not here.
> If I sit still enough for long enough maybe I'll float up to the ceiling and then I could look down on my stupid ugly body self sitting there stupid and ugly (p. 6).

In the original production Leila was played in jeans and a hoodie, in another she wore the hijab. Greig considers issues of staging a matter for the company: 'I don't like to think of it in terms of right or wrong. The play is just a vehicle for the company to explore issues that are of interest and importance to them.'

The issues that are of interest and importance to Leila in the play, and what she articulates in the extract above, are an obsession with media figures whose reality she can only occupy momentarily, when she looks at the glossy images as she cuts herself. Until, of course, Stag Lee comes along and makes her feel the kind of real she longs for: 'I feel like I'm [...] in a story and people are imagining me and wondering what I think' (p. 22). Leila feels real when she and Lee enter the mansion since Blackwater Lodge looks like the images in the magazines where her idea of the 'real' lives. So too does one of the figures from these magazines, temporarily at least: Holly Malone. Holly mirrors Leila's desire to be someone and somewhere else, and cuts herself in Leila's presence, again mirroring Leila's behaviour and telling her 'I wish I was you. / I wish you were me' (p. 44), constantly asking 'Do you know who I am?'.

Everyone in the play is trying to escape from or to a reality, after all. The women escape through self-abuse: Leila and Holly both have 'tribal markings' and Lee's mother self-medicates whenever the 'black dog' bites. Lee's father, Frank, is an alcoholic and Lee attempts to escape his reality with fantasies about who his father is; his nickname and his baseball cap copied from the

Stag tattooed on Frank's body. Finding a postcard, Lee goes in search of the luxury estate depicted, finding instead a ghillie's caravan at the end of a journey he and Leila barely survive. Initially it is Lee who makes everything 'real' for Leila (p. 19) but ultimately it is she who writes a future for Lee, with her, when he threatens suicide as the police catch up with him. Though Lee is initiator of their adventure ('Are you coming or are you coming?'), Leila finds her voice to guide him through their first sexual encounter and uses her promise to wait for him to keep him alive. In Scene Twenty, there are no narrators, just stage directions and Leila and Lee talking directly to one another, Lee telling Leila that her voice is 'beautiful' (p. 58).

In the original production of *Yellow Moon*, for the majority of the play, Leila's internal monologues are spoken by the other actors: a literal rendering of the relationship between authorial voice and character. Like *Yellow Moon, A Slow Air* is a play full of voices, all spoken by the play's two-person cast. All of the characters' dialogue is mediated through Morna and Athol's voices. Thus does Athol give us the words of Bilal Abdullah and Kafeel Ahmed, and of the Rabbani family. The voices of South Asian Scots are spoken by a middle aged white Scot; again – and acknowledging these voices as just a few of the many reproduced by the siblings – the play's form foregrounds the way in which these voices are constructed.

There is a circularity to each of the play's narratives. In *Yellow Moon*, we learn that Frank has fled to the Highlands after he stabs someone to death, just as his fleeing son has done. In *A Slow Air*, Clay's release into the Rabbani home echoes the attack Joshua suffered as a child; the latter setting in motion the events that led to the siblings' silence. Ideas of difference exist as an undercurrent, present but not reconciled, not yet resolved. Like the figures in their family photos, suspended somewhere in the air. The voices heard in these plays aren't speaking Urdu, but there is still present in the narrative the voice of a different Scotland, a future Scotland that echoes Ian Brown's anticipation that articulates both presence and absence at once. We are all of us in the gutter. Anything can happen from here.

Notes

1.   Brown, I., 2011. Allan Ramsay and the invisibility cloak: the historiography of Scottish drama?'. TaPRA, *Annual Conference*. Kingston University, London 7 September 2011. Aspects of the presentation are written as 'Public and Private

Performance: 1650–1800' in Brown, I. ed. 2011. *The Edinburgh Companion to Scottish Drama*. Edinburgh: Edinburgh University Press, pp. 22-40.

2.   'Ankur Productions aims to transform the representation of Black and Minority Ethnic artists and Black and Minority Ethnic communities in the production, consumption and enjoyment of arts and culture in Scotland.' Ankur Productions, 2012. *Vision & Mission* [online] Available at: http://www.ankurproductions.org.uk/#/about-us/vision [Accessed 31 January 2012].

3.   *Yellow Moon*, premiered 29 September 2006 at the Citizens' Theatre, Circle Studio, Glasgow.

4.   Bhabha, H. K. 1994. *The Location of Culture*. London: Routledge, p. 20.

5.   I would like to thank David Greig for his helpful insights into the play and David Harrower for the performance version of *A Slow Air*.

6.   McMillan, J., 2011. Theatre reviews, The Scotsman, [online] 18 May. Available at: http://www.scotsman.com/news/theatre-reviews-dunsinane-a-slow-air-top-table-1-1648977 [Accessed 25 January 2013].

7.   Harrower, D. 2011. *A Slow Air. London*. Faber and Faber, p. 7.

8.   Harrower describes his desire to write 'a little paean to the Edinburgh I remember [...] before the days of the Scottish government, around the time of the constitutional convention, the poll tax marches. There are landmarks I associate with that time. The Mound was always the place you marched up in a 1,000 strong crowd, usually to The Meadows. You'd see Hamish Henderson in Sandy Bell's, it felt like being in touch with the older, more radical Scotland.' news.scotsman.com. 2011. Interview: David Harrower, playwright, *The Scotsman*. [online] 12 May. Available at: http://www.scotsman.com/news/interview-david-harrower-playwright-1-1631362 [Accessed 31 January 2013].

9.   'Athol'd call me a traitor. Aw the great Scottish rock music an you have tae go over the water? / What great Scottish music? Fuckin Runrig? Great singalong band they were, every fuckin word in Gaelic' (p. 27).

10. From Alex Salmond's speech to the annual SNP conference in 1995, quoted by S. Reicher and N. Hopkins, 2001. *Self and Nation*. London: Sage Publications, p. 164.

11. In *The Scotsman*, Harrower says that '[t]he drama that I like is reverberative drama, more akin to poetry which bleeds into you.'

12. Greig, 2007. *Yellow Moon: The Ballad of Leila and Lee*. London: Faber and Faber, p. 4.

13. Greig, D., 2013. (Personal communication, January 2013).

14. Reviewing the original production for the *New York Times*, Charles Isherwood described the character as 'of Arab descent' and the actor as 'the lovely Ms. Chetty [who] has a shy, sidelong smile that touches the heart and an imploring hunger in her dark eyes'. Isherwood, C. 2008. Teenagers Share A Bottle in a Cemetery, and Soon They're on the Run. *New York Times* [online] 30 April. Available at: http://theater.nytimes.com/2008/04/30/theater/reviews/30yell. html [Accessed 25 January 2013].

15. In 1996, August Wilson spoke about the importance for African American actors to have their own parts written by their own playwrights. Wilson, A. 2000. The Ground on Which I Stand. New York: Theatre Communications Group.

Alex Williams

Even the President of the United States Sometimes Stands Naked

Raining. The smell of wet paint on the railing. The woman who fell down
stairs is having a baby. The smell of wet pavement. Time is your dad in a

blue tie. Sundown's blood-orange & cantaloupe tie-dye. The difference
between brain & mind is the time it takes to think. The eye's a dog, time's

a tether. Crows of a murder flock together. Being important is nice but nice
is better. Two red moose and green spruce stitched to a Christmas sweater.

There's nothing good about perfect order, but nothing good about chaos either.
Time is one pricey parking meter. The city is a copper coin slipped through oily

fingers. Philip Levine said 'I do not believe in sorrow. It is just so unAmerican.'
The woman who fell down stairs is now in labor at the university hospital in Ann

Arbor. Snip of scissor. Warm shave cream. The quick scratch of razor
on the back of your neck at the barber's. Time is your father wearing a blue

hat. Life is hairs on a young person's balding head. Ten Black & Tans please.
What's that? That's right. Ten of them. The smell of the dunes & sound of music

from empty rooms. Nothing good about so much weight, but nothing good about
hummingbirds either. Cake. The word, even, is icing-topped and light-and fluffy-

centered. The woman who fell down stairs is dying, but first will give birth to me.
The smell of wet smoke stuck in your throat. Time is my nameless naked daddy.

Sketch of a Woman in the Great Wide Open

What sweet long-awaited relief dabbed sweat-beads from the soft brow of she
who discovered the gate unlocked to a garden she so long wanted to walk in.

The gate was surrounded by thistle & thorn. All of a sudden, her body was foreign.
She forgot the world was just one bunch of words clumped on a vine like so many

kinds of grape. She forgot the tune, the words, the taste. She always knew life spiraled out
from centers like petals, like rays from the same old sun, but when she was ten she

was fascinated by the word 'murder'. They were out for Chinese and her mother was talking
about reading The Shining. She put out a pointer finger and moved it as she spoke through it.

But that is neither there nor here. Now the woman's hand palmed the splintered garden door.
She breathed a short breath. Paused. Breathed again. Pushed. Now she pushes some more.

A Bird in the Shadow of Leaves

Now, the wild green parrots of Telegraph Hill are flown from San Francisco.
Mustangs, Aztecs, Wranglers, Hell's Angels, once vroomed the Embarcadero

but busted flats, abandoned wheels, or crashed years ago. Fruit-stands line
the bayside road, unmanned, overseeing the garbage and unseen street

entertainers who sing and dance in costume to jazz-based groove. Up Route 1,
up north near a famous Napa Valley vineyard and a neon-sour grapefruit grove,

a bird is alive who knows the answer to every question asked. Men, women,
a child once, dedicate their lives to finding this bird who is impossible to find.

She is the mother of all the wild green parrots of Telegraph Hill, not by blood,
but heart, spirit, and spine. The flock of the parrots is a single body and she,

called by some Mother Green Wing, is the breast as well as the fat fertile
belly. She is something somewhere central and crucial, bearing, fruitful,

but essentially impossible to name or faithfully describe. Mother Wing cannot be
named because she has never been seen. They say she exists outside of time –

unborn but alive, flying where redwoods tower, red and wide, leaves lime green,
singing and darting in the canopy, obscured and silenced by a shadow of leaves

so true, so perfect, complete, it doesn't need light to cast itself down –
the shadow sings the song of the self to make new light all its own.

Linda McLean

Extract from *The Uncertainty Files*

The Uncertainty Files is based on interviews recorded while Linda McLean was in residency at the Orchard Project, NY, in June/July 2010. It was commissioned by Paines Plough Theatre Company and produced by Òran Mór in September/October 2010, directed by Charlotte Gwinner. The parts were played by Lesley Hart, Stephen Duffy and Helen Mallon.

Cast:

EL	FEMALE 60
T	MALE 40
D	MALE 35
AM	MALE 33
R	FEMALE 32
MA	FEMALE 30
H	FEMALE 28
JA	MALE 28
AN	MALE 25
MI	FEMALE 24
K	FEMALE 24
EM	FEMALE 23
AF	FEMALE 23

Words in brackets, for example **[fridge]** are sounds.
Italics in brackets, for example s(*elf*) are my best guess at what the word would have been if the person had finished saying it.

This extract begins at Speech Number 3.

3

JA MALE 28

I'm
I
I dated this woman
all spring
and the kind of
one of the central
problems
[car]
of our relationship
is about control
because we're both very controlling
people
but that's
those are big uncertainties
[car]
uh
and the way it was manifest in a little uncertainty is
um
cooking?
when we cook together?
um
like a lot of
back seat
you know
so she'll be making something and I'll say
[truck]
'I think you need to be doing it this way'
[fridge]
um
which
[fridge]
uh

I did that to her with a quiche
and then I ruined the quiche
so
it's become
the verb is now
quiching
to quiche someone

4

K FEMALE 24

I'd always been
certain
even when we fight
I
never
would leave the fight feeling like
screw this I'm
I'm over
over this
um
and when
I guess more recently
I've had these feelings of
um
feelings for
other people ah
um
my ex-girlfriend keeps –
and she's in a relationship too –
she keeps contacting me
um
there – there's just been a
uh
feelings for people that um

that I haven't experienced s-since we've been dating
um
and I mean I guess I've experienced that
in other relationships
but relationships that weren't
right for me? so
it makes me wonder
um
if
this is right
um
and what has changed
and um
and is it normal to have
you know
feelings for other people?
or not tss **[kind of laugh]**
um
because it's not something that I
experienced and I mean I know
people talk about experiencing that all the time
but they also know the relationships that are
right for them
um
and you know
how do you
I'm just uncertain about how to
you know
restart that spark?
that's ss
gone away
um
And so that's kind of
nerve wracking I guess
and hard
because

I don't really know
how I would
it's complicated because I f-feel like I couldn't
not
have her
either
because I want her so much
um
it's just confusing
because um
I wouldn't want
her not to be part of my life
I wouldn't want to
not
live with her
it's just
it's complicated
and like
if I'm already having feelings for
other people
how are we going to go
on for ever?
[fridge]
sometimes I do feel like
um
she's not intimate enough and is it that?
but um
but it didn't
make me think ss
that I wasn't certain and I think
maybe the lack of intimacy's
is what's leading to these
these feelings? but um
we don't
I don't know
ss like

I just don't know
how to
because I've talked with her real often
and it just seems like
like
ss it's not a change she wants to make
and so
I don't really know
how
two
people
go on
for all that time and
not
not
you know
not be intimate with each other

5

AN MALE 25

I – I guess the reason m-my mind is going there is because it's so
eh
now
lying in bed
having this
this conversation with my girlfriend a few
a couple of months ago now
[fridge]
ah
where it
suddenly looked very real that we would
we would
not be together
[fridge]

and we approached that line
and but we both
uh
[fridge]
I just rember remember us both clinging to each other and saying
bye
and that was coming from this place of not knowing
[car passes]
um
who would take care of
us
you know
like like
that next day
we're back out in the world alone
whe-where
are we next going to find love?
um
now
you know
your future
which has started to align
and you
you started to see certain things falling into place
is now a slate again
a blank slate
and so it's that fear
it's just that abyss
that
it's
it
so how that felt was literally like
clinging to a life raft
in
you know
after going overboard

you're clinging to this one thing because the rest is unknown
um
[fridge]
and that was very uh
tightening
it was uh
pulling inward
like I couldn't bring her close enough to me
it was like
what you're
what I ultimately needed was for
to meld **[short laugh]**
just not let
glue her to me so she couldn't go anywhere
um
so that was this
that was like a
vortex
that was like a
force that needed to pull in
certainty
and I needed to grab hold of it

6

H FEMALE 28

I think we know in our gut
and I used to n-not trust that at all
and I used to do like
really
b-totally inconsiderate things
like
cheat on my boyfriend cause I was like
'Mmm, I'm attracted to that guy'
and you know **[laugh]**

just
really awful things
that I knew
in my gut
weren't the right thing to do
but I just wasn't listening to my gut
'cause I was just listening to my like
carnal desires
or my
appetite
you know
or
my ego
which was like
'but you have to'
'hook up with that guy'
'because'
'then y –'
'people will think you're hot or s s'(*omething*)
you know it was like
totally
I was totally out of control
so now I try to listen to my gut instincts
more
there's that tiny voice in your head
that tells you sort of what to do
and it's very small
and you have to be very quiet to listen to it
because the loud voice is like
'GO HOOK UP WITH THAT GUY'
'HE'S HOT'
and you're like
'YEAH'
and then you're like
'but he's not nice
'and he treats me like shit

'and
'he doesn't call me back
'and he only sends me text messages
'and he made fun of
'th-that thing I did
'and
'I don't think so'
but your –
the loud voice –
I
I was dealing with a guy that I was
sort of dating recently
he was NOT NICE to me
and the loud voice in my head kept saying like
'BUT COME ON'
'THERE'S NO ONE ELSE OUT THERE'
'YOU SHOULD GO BACK TO HIM'
and I'm like
I was like
'MmHmm'
'Good idea' **[laugh]**
and then my friend was like
'okay'
'but like'
'what about'
'what does that tiny voice say to you'
'if you're really quiet'
and I really should practise meditation but I'm
too
scared right now
I don't want to do it that much
but I'm really interested in it and
I think if
you know
if you sit quietly in meditation and
try to listen to that tiny voice

it usually tells you
the opposite of what the loud voice
and it just says
'there's someone better out there for you
than that mean guy
you don't need to be with him'
there's no way there would be no more pain
cause we had two dates
and after those dates I was s(o)
like so-o sad
and I was crying
and I was
so hurt by some of the things he had said and done
and I still wanted to go out on another date with him
really weird
but now I have
after talking to her about it
and talking to my other friends who were like
'you were really sad'
like
sometimes we really need other people's perspective
to help us become certain
because my head is like
'but he's cute'
'and he lives really close by'
'so you guys can like'
'watch a movie when you're bored'
and it's like w –
we really need our friends to
help us find our
certainty
and all my friends were like
'don't go out with guy'

7

JA MALE 28

I was just wondering if there's certainty in
[bike]
um
huh
you see
I don't think that another person can be your certainty
like
I think that that's dangerous
to
to become dependent on a person
but I think
PEOPLE
can be a certainty
like
that we exist
that
we
build
these things
that we have created civilisations
history
I think there's been a historical
em
evolution – evolution of man
[fridge, car]
as a
u(*ser*)
like as a
a
builder of things
I think there's certainty in that
like

I find
comfort in that
[fridge]
and community.

8

R FEMALE 32

I wanted to be religious so-o much
I wanted to KNOW
[boys' laughter nearby]
and
and
more I think I just wanted a community
and I think part of
um
the certainty is
you find your people when you're certain
like you know
that it's
um
this religion or that religion
then
then
you belong with those people
and you know
um
you're
and you're righteous about
s-some
politics
you know
and I think that's what I was looking
I was looking for a certainty that these are my people
and

I think being
mixed race and being a family that's all
um
mixed race and displaced and
and
every
part of our family
is
um
is displaced because of World War Two and that's how we all came together
so there's a lot of
uh
not longing/belonging and running away
and
uh
and
uh
[door slams hard shut]
disowning past

9

MI FEMALE 24

I
I've never been able to have a cat because my Dad's allergic
but whenever I went to my Great Aunt or someone else that has a cat
I'm able to like
immediately get them to like me
like I'll be able to pet them in just so
that they'll start purring for me
uh
which like
especially with my Great Aunt
she always has like a cat

at one point
um
and like
she always
she always has at least one cat
and
I mean she hasn't
she's never had more than two since I've known her
but she loves cats
em
so like with one like
Goofy
she always says when I come
'See if you'
'See if you can get him to purr for you'
and like
and I can
it's just like
patting him
he's just like
likes me
uh
um
and I feel like that way about dogs too.

Roddy Lumsden

Tact

Mid-afternoon and I enact a policy, the elementary
one against ambiguity. So, in this park, it's simple
beasts at first: a squirrel is a sculpted pigling, nut
in mouth; a cinnamon-headed fly romps on a
slab; a blackbird scraiks in the hedgerow, delving
reddest berries, ones which tease from me the giddy
painters' words for scarlets; a toadstool, stillest of
brutes, stirs uncautious concepts – the prettier of
two sisters, or the prettily filmy phases of a bruise
(tact is not yet ambiguity). Then, wild coriander (the
local word a cheekful of hornets), a violet lozenge
of a butterfly, and another an inch off lemon. And
at last, what was missing from your bestiary: a grey-
bellied rodent flossing the old teeth of a dry wall;
new lovers who laugh at they don't know what;
some cousin of the waxwing which halves the space
between maple and beech, heads to where policy
and concept meld or melt, to the self's sluice, where
it settles to drink.

Farewell to Conchiglie

(Eype – West Bay – Eype)

I most feared being asked what I most wanted.

I stood on the bar bridge and looked up the Lyme river.

A combo jazzed out one of one too many songs named 'You
Belong to Me'.

I knew you could have minestrone without the pasta (but turn up
that white pepper).

I thought of Kona, unable to speak her name in Portugal.

I roamed slit-eyed past huts selling cones of chips and cones
of ice cream.

There was rye in my stomach and it was touch and go.

Three good things: a skipper butterfly, a tub of brown shrimps
and a kissing gate.

Weymouth was hazy and behind me, if you see what I mean.

Such distance is neverending, neverending.

I was fairly sure I would die without jet-skiing.

I wanted to patent shingle walking as a remedy for gout.

I misted over when people talked of novels, or movies, or other assorted fictions, or me.

I climbed the steepness until it steeped the other way.

I thought of Charlie also steeping in the sun, slowly going the colour of my *Fab India* shirt.

And my friends weekending in Biarritz, Dom sharing with Al because he was *less grubby* than Nick or Gerard.

A boy made of his hands a neverending ladder for a ladybird.

And there ahead, at Sevelons, was Annie, perhaps with another 'good rope story' ready.

Her father's self-portraits were on the cover of every broadsheet.

Another father was teaching his young son to piss with the wind.

Three bad things: a fierce rabbit skull, a charred log, gnat legs jolting on my Factor 15ed nape.

Not that people talked often of me in my presence.

I was a lord of the flies and now I'd blown the conch.

I never cared for pasta anyway. My failure to admit that is to my shame.

I sent a shock of water down into my well.

Piss with the wind? Frankly I didn't give a damn.

Old local proverb: *on a shingle strand there are no shells*. Its meaning lost in time.

Some times there are no pros and cons, just cons and cons.

But I did give a damn. I always had.

Women in Paintings

The masters laboured – *all the hours of the clock* –
to clone the ringlets of a marchioness or pull
a cape of dark around the head of an ecstatic saint.

Portraiteers talked low and long to captive sitters,
so Boleyn's swan neck can still be kissed, Jill
persist in a steel blue frock, the year my parents met.

And in *Sous Bois*, Corot threw down a lilac twister
of a sunstreak, through which the bonneted girl
is ever about to step, daydreaming of candied fruit.

Day yields to dusk. The artful lie takes awful work.
We strive words from the loath core of our will:
You will be loved again. Everything'll be all right.

Pulegone

What am I still into?
Knowing I grow so slowly,
that summer is coming,

and time – *only another liar* –
will try to hide the wall
where wallflowers thrive.

That, and the squall
of soft-loud-soft,
the catmint of mismelody

for which I'll drool and roll.
That, and luckless girls
of sulky appetite

who'd write my story
in their wombs,
their picas brimming.

Zinnie Harris

Extract from *The Garden*

The Garden was originally produced as part of The World is Too Much With Us season at the Traverse theatre, then as an Òran Mór/ Traverse A Play, a Pie and a Pint season.

Cast: JANE Anne Lacey MAC Sean Scalan Director: Zinnie Harris

A couple living in a high-rise flat in a baked-out world discover a plant growing through the lino in their kitchen. Plants have long since stopped growing so they don't know what to make of it. They rip it up, but it grows back. Then they realise it is an apple tree…

Scene One

A small kitchen in a high-rise flat.
Old lino on the floor, peeling paint.
The heat is almost unbearable.
A woman, JANE, is sitting in a folding chair.
A man, MAC, comes into the room and takes off his tie.

MAC   I wouldn't mind if I hadn't been part of it from the beginning. From like what, three years ago? Before that even when we were back in the States. Before then even. Five years maybe. Before Manning anyway. Before Peters, Leinher, all of them. Christ this shirt is sweaty, before McClennan who they have promoted by the way. Does this stink? Can you smell it from there?

JANE   No.

MAC   I had to run three blocks for the bus, even then I couldn't get a
       seat. You should put more buses on, I said, this number of people,
       that's what it's about you see, Manning sees it the wrong way. It's
       about people on buses. It's about the day-to-day, yeah sure the long
       term future but one has to get through the day-to-day to get there.
       You don't get to tomorrow without passing through today. I told
       him that, he didn't like it. It's too straightforward for him. He likes
       a calculation. Fuck the calculations, it's about buses, it's about water.
       It's about…
       Fuck, sometimes I don't even know what it's about.
       Any beer?

JANE   In the fridge.

He goes to the fridge.

JANE   Bottom shelf.
       It's not cold.

MAC   Do you want one?

JANE   No.

MAC   Manning's never liked me anyway.

JANE   That's not true.

MAC   In the old days maybe.

JANE   He and his wife have been around here.

MAC   Not for years.

JANE   Months.

MAC   They left soon enough.

JANE   He likes you fine.

MAC   So why shove me off the sub-committee? Took me aside today, honestly Jane, took me right to one side, everyone around but low voice. Like this, shook my hand, said thank you for the work etc etc.

JANE   Well that's good.

MAC   It's a brush off. Said I could be on the main committee, I said what about the sub, he said the sub's for the seniors, seniors my arse. Is Leinher, is Rogers, are they senior to me? We all know it's the sub committee that's where the action is, where the important stuff happens. What are they doing sitting there? Three years, more even, I said to him. Three years of my life, ask my wife, I don't do anything else, haven't done anything else, every part of me –
And we are grateful.
That's what he said.
Hand on my arm. Fat wrists.
Grateful.
Fucking hell.

He opens the beer.

JANE   I always liked his wife.

MAC   Don't.

[beat]

Mac drinks the beer.

[pause]

MAC   Shit, what is this?

74

JANE   All that's left.
           The electricity went off.

MAC   When?

JANE   Earlier.

MAC   You went downstairs?

JANE   Everyone went downstairs. It was crowded.

MAC   Shit.

JANE   The Cranfords are packing.

MAC   We're not moving.

JANE   They say anywhere's better than here.

MAC   Everywhere is the same.

JANE   Don't shout at me.

MAC   I didn't shout.

[beat]

MAC   I didn't shout.

JANE   You always shout when I mention moving.

MAC   Moving isn't going to solve anything. You want to move, we should have done it three years back, before the committees, the subs.

JANE   Everyone's going.

MAC   They'll be back.

JANE   Even the Woodies.

MAC   Ivan?

JANE   Yes.

MAC   He's moving his family?

JANE   You don't know what it's like, in the heat. During the day.

MAC   They'll be back.
        Of course they will. I wish I was as sure of many things as I am of
        that.

JANE   They've got another baby on the way.

MAC   That's nice.

[beat]

MAC   Anyway I've got another meeting with Manning, so I can put it all
        to him them. If I can get a moment alone with him away from the
        others, try to get him to remember what it is I've been doing. Notice.
        Did you want a beer?

JANE   No.

MAC   Did you already say?

JANE   I said.

MAC   Sorry. If I lose the job…

JANE   You won't.

[beat]

MAC   What did you do today?

JANE   I went downstairs.
I came back up.
I rinsed out the sheets.

MAC   The water came on?

JANE   Briefly.
I cleaned the floor.

MAC   Looks good.

JANE   There's a bump in the lino.

MAC   Where?

JANE   Over there.
I thought it was maybe just a buckle from the heat.

MAC   Here?

JANE   Yes.
But it's not.
There's something under it.

MAC   How could something get under it?

JANE   I don't know.

He gets down to have a look.

MAC   It's just a buckle from the heat.

JANE   I thought that.
        I noticed it yesterday, but it's bigger today.

MAC   How can it be bigger today?

JANE   I'm just telling you what I saw. The facts as I saw them.

The man stamps on it.

JANE   I wondered if it was a mouse.

[beat]

JANE   Or some kind of creature.

MAC   A mouse?

JANE   It could be. Something small like that.

MAC   Here?

JANE   I've heard of it.

MAC   If it's a mouse I'll take it in to Manning I tell you. If it's a mouse I'll
        be back on the sub.

He gets down and sniffs it.

MAC   Nah.

JANE   It doesn't matter anyway.
        It was just you asked. Just you showed an interest so I told you.
        I could have told you about the crack in the bedroom ceiling that I
        am following with a pencil. Or the smell that comes from the drains
        when the old man flushes the toilet. What are you doing?

MAC   Getting some tools.

JANE   Mac –

MAC   What, we just going to leave this thing to mystery?

JANE   It's a small bump in the lino.

MAC   There's no such thing.

JANE   You're going to dismantle the kitchen?

MAC   Of course I'm not.
        I'm just going to peel back a corner of the floor.

He starts to take pins out of the floor.

JANE   You remember when we found that toad, back in Queensland?
        You took up a floorboard.

MAC   It was a frog.

JANE   It hopped about the kitchen.

MAC   I don't remember that part.

JANE   Right before you ran it through with a chair.

MAC   Can you help me with this?
        Take the other end?

She does.
Together they peel back the lino.
They look at what is underneath.

JANE   Huh.

MAC   Well well.

JANE   How the devil did that get there?
        What you doing?

MAC   Pulling it up.

JANE   Do you have to?

MAC   We are five floors up.

JANE   It's a living thing.

MAC   It's a weed.
        If it's growing here, it will be putting its roots in the concrete. You
        know what that can do to a structure, we've already got cracks.

She stops him.

JANE   But when did you last see something that… that fresh colour. I know
        there is grass, but the grass…

MAC   I've got a shirt that colour.

JANE   Just let me look at it.

MAC   It's a weed.

JANE   Nothing ever grows in our house.

MAC   That's not true.

JANE   Everything dies, but this…

MAC   It will kill the building. Get its roots into the drains. You're always
        complaining about where we live.

You can pull it up if you like.

[beat]

JANE   Do we have to?

MAC   Yes.

JANE   Couldn't we move it? Put it in a little pot and try to grow it on the
window ledge?

MAC   As you said, everything dies in our house.

He rips it up.

MAC   It shouldn't bother us anymore now.

**He throws it to one side and starts to put the lino back down.
She picks it up and looks at it.**

JANE   If we knew what it was, we could eat it.

MAC   I don't think so.

JANE   Might be a lettuce.

MAC   Under the floor boards?

JANE   Or a tomato.
We could have dropped a little pip.

MAC   You get these ideas. I don't know where they come from.
It's a weed.

JANE   Even a weed has a name.

MAC   Not all weeds.
        Weeds by definition are things that are a nuisance.
        It would have strangled the building.

JANE   I'm going to taste it.

MAC   You'll be sick.

She tastes it.
Bitter.
He laughs.

JANE   Maybe it was going to produce a flower then. A flower I could wear
        in my hat.
MAC   Since when have you had a hat?

[beat]

MAC   Put it in the bin. It's dead now anyway.

JANE   I wish we had a garden.
        I could throw it out of the window, it could land and a whole forest
        could grow.

MAC   Please Jane, you have to get these ideas out of your head.
        We are doing our best. No one has gardens. If you want a garden,
        you have to move three families to get one. You want people or you
        want gardens?

She puts the plant in the bin.

JANE   I don't know.

MAC   People are good.

JANE   Are they?

MAC   What are the Woodies going to call their new baby when it arrives?

She shrugs.

MAC   You didn't ask?

JANE   I get confused with their existing kids.

He puts the pins back in.

MAC   Pass the hammer.

She does.
He bangs.

MAC   If you are really bothered I could take it to Manning.

JANE   And say what?

MAC   See what he makes of it. He has all those guys working in the lab. Over half an inch of lino. No water. Whatever it was, it was a survivor.

JANE   Do you remember that night you got so drunk and peed on the floor?

MAC   Why are you bringing that up?

JANE   I'm just trying to remember where the wee went.

MAC   I had a temperature.

JANE   I know.

MAC   Between the wine and the virus.

JANE   I think you were there. Crashed out somewhere over on that side of
       the room.
       If the wee were to have run.

MAC   You saying it's my fault?

JANE   I'm saying it's something.

MAC   Something, what do you mean?

JANE   Something came from us, after all.

MAC   You'll have to clean the floor again tomorrow.

JANE   I don't mind.

MAC   Is there any more beer?

JANE   I'll get you one.

MAC   Do you want one?

JANE   No.

MAC   Did you already say?

JANE   I already said.

Scene Two

**Jane is alone in the kitchen. In front of her, coming out of the lino in
exactly the same position as before, is the plant.**
It has grown and is now between one and two feet tall.

JANE   If it were three or four in the morning, I would say I was asleep. Five
       at a push, or late say eleven or twelve. One in the morning. I can

sleep through anything. I can sleep and move around and see things. I could be here and talking to you and be asleep. I can be in bed making love to Mac and asleep. I can be standing in the street with the rain on my face and asleep. Naked in a train station and asleep.
But in my own kitchen in the middle of the afternoon?
If I'm asleep I must be ill.
I don't sleep in the afternoons. Not anymore. So if you are a dream, a trick. I know it's the afternoon because I had my lunch. I sat outside. Mac says the sun light is good for me, so I went out.
I'm not ill.
By the way. Not at all.

She reaches out to touch a leaf. She doesn't quite dare.

JANE   We put the lino back down.
He ripped out your roots.
I don't want to be ill again. If I'm ill then I have to go back on those bloody things. And see doctors and
I'm not going to do all of that because of a bloody plant.
I'm going to make some coffee.
Coffee will wake me up.

She turns her back to it. Pours some coffee.
Turns back around.

JANE   You are going to have to go. If somehow we left a root last time, he's going to be more thorough this time. He'll say we can't have a plant growing in the middle of the kitchen. He won't be happy, he likes a job to be done.
It's a crazy place to grow, what are you thinking? Why don't you try outside? There are acres outside where everyone would be delighted. Biology is supposed to count against the most stupid. By all rights you should be ripped up. It's a stupid place to be.
You don't deserve to turn into an adult plant, have little ones of your own. You chose bad soil.
Plus you ruined our lino.

[beat]

JANE   I'll get some scissors, is that what you want?

[beat]

JANE   Weed.

[beat]

She drinks the coffee.
She puts it down.

JANE   You are going to have to have gone by the time he gets home.
He'll blame me. And we'll fight and I don't want that.
We fight too much as it is.

She picks up some scissors.
She approaches the plant.

JANE   I'm not a gardener.
I'm not much of anything.

She chops a leaf off the plant.

JANE   You've only yourself to blame.

She chops another leaf off. And another.
Soon she has chopped off all the leaves except one.
She plays with the pile of leaves.
She is about to chop the final leaf off.
She pauses. Then she chops that one off too.

JANE   Sorry.

Ross Wilson

After Work

With tired limbs stretching
and a yawn snatching words
like a bird swallowing flies,
and the duvet warm over skin,
and the soft arm draping
a meal-swollen belly
like a belt buckling him
into dream, he forgot
about the alarm, silent
as a sniper under cover
of mug and book –
the cold dark set in its sites.

Numbers

8 am – Home: a ninety year old woman
watched him move, agile as a young animal,
trolley to table, table to trolley, lifting cutlery,
milk jugs, sugar... a salt-shaker fell
scattering salt on the floor. He bent to lift it,
on one foot, no problem, and got on
with his work, the old woman
watching intently from a wheel-chair –
the eyes of a predator pursuing prey.

1 pm – an NHS nurse caught him
on his break, asked if he wanted a health check:
I know you're young but
my door is open to all staff.
Age, glucose, cholesterol, blood pressure,
weight, height, BMI, waist...
numbers added up to what he was
as the nurse spoke of
The Sick Man of Europe...

6 pm – his wage slip told him
what a month's work added up to,
and habit made sure those figures
quickly began to sift through
the plastic between his fingers,
harvesting tobacco, lager, cigarette
papers, hash, fast food, chocolate,
and a lottery ticket.

7 pm – home: the letterbox waiting
like a loyal dog: bills in its mouth;
numbers he didn't bother adding up,
numbers he stuck on a hi-fi top.
He licked cigarette papers, looked up over
an un-Hoovered floor, at numbers on a screen
that didn't match the numbers on the arm-
rest like a dream going up in the smoke
of the ash-tray that kept them down.

Ian Brown

More to Come: Forty Years of the Scottish Society of Playwrights

In the autumn of 1973 a group of around twenty-five playwrights gathered in an upper room at the Netherbow Theatre in Edinburgh. Called by a circular sent out by Ena Lamont Stewart, Hector MacMillan and John Hall, the meeting grew out of a sense of frustration among Scottish playwrights with existing methods of dealing with theatre managements, settling fees and supporting new writing. Several of those who attended were members of the Writers Guild which at that time seemed very much focused on other forms of writing and, so far as drama was concerned, with broadcast media and film; some had recently broken through into being produced onstage but, despite their success, shared the view that some fresh initiative was needed to develop support for playwriting and to act as a new channel for playwrights to speak collectively.

One might have expected that the debate in the room would be passionate. It was. But it was not self-centred, or not very. It was primarily concerned for the future of Scottish theatre, and playwriting within it, arising from a perception that there was in many Scottish theatres a lack of proper concern for new writing. The Traverse, now rightly seen as the national new writing company, was then far from committed to new writing, let alone Scottish new writing. Its artistic director Mike Ockrent, like his predecessor Mike Rudman, seemed more interested in possible West End links or presenting European classics. And while the Citizens' was undoubtedly producing work of high quality, at that stage it was showing no interest in producing new writing, let alone new Scottish work (though it was soon to nurture the work of Robert David Macdonald). One playwright actually walked out of the meeting in protest at the suggestion that the Citizens, set up to support *inter alia* new writing, might not be fulfilling its original remit. In fact no one had objected to the aesthetic of the Citizens' artistic director Giles Havergal, or contested his right to develop his own artistic policy – the issue was how to secure a proper place in Scottish theatre for new Scottish writing. To this end, the meeting resolved to establish a society of playwrights dedicated to supporting theatre and playwriting in Scotland. The priorities identified that night remain enshrined in the Scottish Society of Playwrights' constitution, as does its overarching intent: 'to promote the development and production of theatre-making in Scotland and to act for playwrights in Scotland in all matters affecting them'.

The model for the Society's organisation – brought to the meeting's attention, as I recall, by Hector MacMillan – was that of the recently formed Society of Irish Playwrights. The meeting, agreeing that the way forward was to found a Society with a similar remit, set about creating a committee to steer its foundation. To my astonishment, Ena Lamont Stewart – whom I had never met until that day – proposed me as Chair on the grounds that 'this young man sitting in front of me seems to talk some sense'. Such was her prestige in that room that her proposal was carried *nem con*, although in retrospect I cannot help thinking that, given the work to be undertaken, my colleagues were pleased someone was so gullible as to take on the role. I was then just twenty-eight with only three or four significant productions, although two had been at the Royal Lyceum and another for the Edinburgh Festival.

Given that we had adopted the Irish model, someone suggested that the new organisation should be called the 'Society of Scottish Playwrights'. I offered the thought that this might seem a little exclusive – how would we define 'Scottish', by residence, or birth, or what? A consensus emerged that we should create a 'Scottish Society of Playwrights' – that is, one working for the interests of Scotland, welcoming any playwright working in Scotland; as well as those who perceived themselves as Scottish working furth of the country. The qualification for full membership of the Society remains the same to this day:

> open to Scots playwrights, wherever resident, or playwrights resident in Scotland, who wish to promote their work in the theatre, and who have written substantial texts requiring the services of actors for performance

in the theatre/radio/television/film and who have had at least one such text publicly and professionally performed.

The committee charged with drafting the constitution comprised Hector MacMillan, Ada F. Kay and myself. We circulated draft after draft among ourselves till we had one we felt ready to bring to the members – and after two members' drafting meetings, late in 1973 the constitution was established. To manage the Society's affairs, a Council was established whose first members included – besides Ena Lamont Stewart, Ada F. Kay, Hector MacMillan, John Hall and me – well-established playwrights like Joan Ure and Donald Mackenzie.

Under this Council's guidance, the SSP quickly became recognised as a co-ordinated voice for playwrights, an advocate of the value of a healthy Scottish theatre, and a playwriting development and promotional agency. One of its first initiatives was to set up workshops to develop new plays on the model of the Eugene O'Neill Theater Center's US National Playwrights' Conference in Connecticut. We also wanted to develop information and publishing strands to our operation. Within six months of our foundation we obtained a grant of £10,000 from the Scottish Arts Council. In this, we were facilitated by the encouragement of the SAC's Drama Director, John Faulkner, perhaps the most progressive and creative individual to have held that post, and its dynamic Director, Sandy Dunbar. To put that grant in perspective, in 2010 terms it equated under the Retail Prices Index to £94,300 and under the Average Earnings Index to £153,000. It is hard to see how, in contemporary conditions, a body of artists less than six months old could achieve such levels of support, however high its members' standing. Those were different times and for the first twelve years of its existence the SSP received SAC funding annually.

This funding meant that, besides such tasks as negotiating the first national contract for playwrights with the Federation of Scottish Theatre and representing playwrights in dispute with theatre managements, the Society could act as a major development agency for playwrights, and in those early years it was also very active in pressing for the Traverse to be a new writing theatre. Without the SSP's advocacy the Traverse might have chosen a new writing ethos, but perhaps not – there was resistance to the SSP campaign from those who took the attitude that European writing must be, *ipso facto*, 'international', and Scottish writing, however internationalist in outlook or dramatic influence must be, *ipso facto*, 'parochial'. It is a mark of how thinking has changed, not least under the impact of the work of the SSP, that today one rarely, if ever, hears such a cringing adjective applied to contemporary Scottish theatre or its new writing.

It was not until the arrival of Chris Parr in the mid-1970s that the Traverse, with the general support of theatre-lovers, dedicated itself to new work as a central focus of its operation. The SSP model of playwrights' workshops evolved – it is now recognised and used throughout the UK (I have written in detail elsewhere[1] of the generational succession – from the O'Neill original, through the SSP in the 1970s – that meant that English bodies adopted the Scottish model, initially developed in England in 1982 through the North West Playwrights' Workshops). It is no exaggeration to say that every playwright development agency now operating in England, Wales and Northern Ireland is directly descended from the initial experiments of the SSP in the period 1974 to the mid-1980s. Indeed, the SSP's overall 1970s operational model is in many ways replicated by Playwrights' Studio Scotland, a phenomenon we will come to later.

It is worth noting how quickly the SSP, at first regarded with suspicion by theatre managements – what were those pesky playwrights up to? – became a focus of exemplary collaboration. After all, the SSP's first aim always was the good of Scottish theatre at large, for without that, how can any playwright hope to benefit adequately? The SSP-FST contract was drawn up by a theatre director, Stephen MacDonald, working collaboratively with a playwright, Hector MacMillan. MacDonald's new writing policies as Director at Dundee Rep (1973–76) and at the Royal Lyceum (1976–79) are legendary for bringing major writers to main stages – at the Lyceum, as much as a third of his programme comprised new Scottish plays. He was committed to fostering a healthy playwriting environment, understanding just how fundamental it is to a healthy theatre culture. The SSP-FST contract recognises that the need for adequate working conditions and, for example, rehearsal attendance payments are as necessary for playwrights as they are for actors. It prevails as the national standard minimum terms agreement in Scotland.

In the 1970s and early 1980s the SSP published important but neglected texts such as Roddy McMillan's *All in Good Faith*, offered members at-cost copying, and published a newsletter which developed in time into *Scottish Theatre News*. Its first administrator, Linda Haase, and her successor, Charles

Hart, both provided outstanding service; Linda went on to help found the Tron Theatre and Charles became a legendary New Writing Officer of the Arts Council in England for over fifteen years from the late 1980s.

Around 1980 the SSP took a fateful decision for the best of reasons, but with ambivalent results. Despite opposition from longstanding members and senior figures including Eddie Boyd and Donald Mackenzie, it was decided to follow the example of the radical Theatre Writers Union in England and extend associate membership to playwrights who were not yet professionally produced. This was intended to encourage and support developing playwrights. Boyd and Mackenzie argued that, while that was an admirable objective, such a decision would dilute the impact of the SSP as the professional organisation for professional playwrights. Nonetheless, what seemed the more inclusive decision was made and associate membership was instituted.

The unintended consequence was that inexperienced playwrights with free access to SSP copying and script-binding facilities identical to that previously enjoyed only by experienced professionals started to flood theatres with their scripts. The arrival of a new script in the SSP binding had come to signify that work of a certain quality could be anticipated but there now came a wave of submissions that did nothing to enhance the prestige of that livery. SSP workshops open to experienced and inexperienced playwrights alike were clearly developmental and, in a sense, experimental, and so they might reasonably present work that was less than successful – but there were very different implications when a script in the SSP binding could not be immediately trusted to be worth considering. SSP publications continued to offer a wide service to Scottish theatre. *Scottish Theatre News* earned a feisty reputation for not pulling its punches, which did not always make it popular with some theatre folk or funders, but the general opinion was that it was none the worse for that. However, the move to extend the copying service to less than fully achieved plays and allow them to emerge into the market under the SSP's aegis led to an erosion of confidence in the SSP's standards.

Having served as Chair between 1973 and 1975, I was re-elected in 1984 at a time when Arts Councils north and south of the Border were reconsidering their priorities. In England, the notorious *Glory of the Garden* strategy report was threatening the survival of many theatre organisations, although the Arts Council did pull back from its most foolish proposals. (Indeed, when I served between 1986 and 1994 as Drama Director in England, part of my time was engaged in undoing some of the harm *The Glory of the Garden* had caused.) The SAC produced its own version of *The Glory of the Garden*, presenting a rethink of its funding priorities and proposing the withdrawal of funding from what it called 'support services' in favour of 'direct provision'.

As it happened, one of the first letters I received after election in June 1984 was from the SAC. I thought it must be a letter of congratulations but when I opened it I saw it was notification of intention to withdraw funding of the SSP from 1985. Despite widespread protests from the theatre profession north and south of the Border the SAC persisted in its intent, impervious to the fact that support for playwrights through the SSP was in fact direct provision. In 1985 the SSP had to close down its workshop, publishing and copying activities – at the time we predicted that the SAC would come to miss the Society's wide-ranging services and would seek a way of recreating them. Meantime, the SSP concentrated on its primary role of representing the playwrights of Scotland. While the Society's funding had more or less kept pace with its level when first granted, only part of its funding went to provide a post of Literary Director (Scotland), which was filled by Tom McGrath. He brilliantly executed the role of developing young playwriting talent, acting as mentor and dramaturg for them.

It has to be said that in the light of these upheavals some discussion circled the question of the continuing viability of the SSP. As Chair I argued – along with many members, including, prominently, Peter Arnott, who had recently joined – that we still could have a vibrant future and represent the interests of playwrights. In order to fulfil the role of a professional union, we realised we had to withdraw the category of associate member. In effect, from being a development agency in the way we operated, the SSP became a union and was soon to join the STUC, of which it remains a member, one of its smaller unions.

This shift of focus opened interesting new avenues of operation. In 1986, as the SSP negotiator I joined forces with representatives of the Writers' Guild and Theatre Writers' Union in establishing our first national agreement with the Theatrical Management Association for the benefit of Scottish playwrights presenting work in England and Wales. The SSP remains a co-signatory to this agreement and in 2010–11 was involved in renegotiating its terms and confirming the extended life of the agreement, which sits alongside and with equal status to the SSP-FST national agreement.

A second new avenue was taken forward by Chris Hannan, my successor as Chair after I stood down in 1987: a survey was sent out to members to establish the average length of time that was involved in writing a play, because the level of commission fees had slipped in the inflationary times since the mid-1970s, and by the late 1980s the standard rate was approximately £2,400. Taking into account the range of individual practice, the survey revealed that the writing of a play required around nine months. Setting this against the income of other theatre workers, it seemed indefensible that nine months' work should generate such a low fee for playwrights but negotiations failed to achieve a substantial increase in the commissioning fee and in 1991 the SSP called a playwrights' strike. Although our claim for a commission fee of £6,000 was regarded in some quarters as an extraordinary request, the impact of the refusal of Scottish playwrights to submit scripts to Scottish theatres concentrated minds; it soon came to be recognised that there had been excessive erosion of rates over the years and a fee of £5,500 was settled on. After the changes instituted in the mid-1980s and its successively negotiation of the TMA contract in 1985–86, the SSP had clearly established itself as the voice of playwrights' interests in Scotland and it went on representing the interests of playwrights throughout Scotland and abroad, maintaining positive relations with theatre management organisations north and south of the Border. The SSP has always been more than simply a negotiating body. For example, it held a conference in Inverness for northern-based playwrights (1999), produced the first authoritative directory of Scottish playwrights (2001) and in 2005 mounted the successful Gathering of Playwrights at the Gateway Theatre. At the Gathering, organised by the late Bill Findlay, several generations of Scottish playwrights reviewed developments in Scottish theatre since 1973 and a popular DVD recording of proceedings was subsequently published.

By the turn of the century the impact of Tom McGrath's fine work as Literary Manager was recognised and there was a surge of debate as to the best way to carry forward playwright support and development. As predicted back in 1984, it had become necessary to 'reinvent' the SSP's development programmes – or at least find ways of fulfilling most of their functions by other means. In 2000 SAC Drama Officer Nikki Axford produced an options appraisal, drawing on a reallocation of the funding of Tom McGrath's post and seeking additional funding. Tom McGrath himself was fully involved in this process, which led to further consultations over the next two years. As part of those, a small working party that included the Drama Director David Taylor (Nikki Axford having moved on in 2001 to become Chief Executive of Pitlochry Festival Theatre), Tom McGrath, Philip Howard of the Traverse Theatre, and, from the SSP, Peter Arnott and myself met regularly to consider ways forward. We had the example of the SSP's pre-1985 and the O'Neill Center's long-time work always on the table. The SAC then employed Faith Liddell, a former Director of the Edinburgh International Book Festival, to consult further with playwrights, theatre companies and educational institutions. From these cumulative discussions, Playwrights' Studio Scotland emerged in 2004.

The SSP, with its clearly defined representative role for the profession, mainly in negotiations, public debate and union representational matters, has enjoyed excellent relations with the Playwrights' Studio, which has a developmental, mentoring and advocacy role. For example, in the mid-2000s the SSP, led by Nicola McCartney, negotiated with managements across Scotland best practice guidelines for dramaturgs; these now stand as a model for the rest of the UK. It also reached an agreement with the National Theatre of Scotland, when it was established, on playwrights' remuneration. It continued to represent the interests of playwrights as body, making submissions to the Cultural Commission and contributing fully, both as a body and through individual members, to the debate about the founding of Creative Scotland and to the more recent debate about that body's conduct of its business. For its part, the Playwrights' Studio has established a lively programme of activities that serves Scottish theatre and its playwrights outstandingly. Both organisations work in harmony, recently coming together to prepare hard evidence for the 2012 Theatre Review for Creative Scotland, led by Christine Hamilton, which has been widely welcomed for its rigour and honesty. It is striking that the first two major things it found to celebrate about Scottish theatre were that:

- New work is the lifeblood of Scottish theatre – often, although not always, this starts with the playwright;
- Scottish theatre has an international reach – again usually with new work.

The international reputation of Scottish theatre, not to mention the prominence and quality of its new work and its playwrights, has been consistently supported and developed by the SSP. Over the last four decades the SSP, launched in that upstairs room at the Netherbow, has served Scottish theatre well. Its work is widely known abroad and it is unquestionably the collective representative voice of playwrights in Scotland. Over the years, however, the SSP has not only been involved in playwright support in formal ways. It has a reputation for lacking self-importance – as Peter Arnott put it in a recent (23 January) email:

> the social aspect of the society has been very important. We've always welcomed the stranger and made them even stranger by association… writing is a lonely business, and part of our job has always been support for individuals as individuals… not just as writers…

The inclusiveness Peter Arnott identifies is important: members include not just Scotland's major playwrights, but many of the rising generation. The Society also recognises the giants on whose shoulders contemporary Scottish playwrights stand. Since the mid-1970s, it has appointed as lifetime Honorary Presidents, senior playwrights whose work has changed the face of Scottish theatre, the first two being Robert McLellan and Ena Lamont Stewart and the current Honorary President being Hector MacMillan. Yet the SSP does not rest on its laurels. Last September the Society raised funding from Creative Scotland for two weeks of translation workshops in Glasgow. Under the title *Translating Texts: Transforming Potential*, Alan Mackendrick worked with German translator Kevin Rittberger on his recently produced *Finished with Engines* and Catherine Grosvenor with Polish translator Grzegorz Stosz on her *Gabriel*. This project, again with the co-operation of the Playwrights' Studio, allowed the scripts to be explored and translated with a view to production in mainland Europe.

Such public activities, complementing the SSP's negotiation and representative functions, continue, and in the week of 8 April 2013 at the Traverse Theatre, the SSP – in association with the Traverse and the Saltire Society – will present five days of events marking its fortieth and the Traverse's fiftieth anniversaries. Each day from Monday to Thursday, events curated respectively by myself, Peter Arnott, Nicola McCartney and Douglas Maxwell will cover a decade of the SSP's existence. Panels of playwrights, practitioners and observers will provide an overview of the work of that decade and each day will conclude with a playreading of a play, chosen by Orla McLoughlin, that was premièred at the Traverse in the relevant period. Rounding off this exploration and celebration of the last forty years of playwriting in Scotland, the Friday event, sponsored by the Saltire Society, will debate the future of playwriting in Scotland. Clearly as it heads into its fifth decade, the SSP continues to look upwards, outwards and forwards.

Notes

1. Ian Brown, 'Playwrights' workshops of the Scottish Society of Playwrights, the Eugene O'Neill Center and their long term impact in the UK', *International Journal of Scottish Theatre and Screen* 4.2 (2011), pp. 35-50 at http://journals.qmu. ac.uk/index.php/IJOSTS/article/view/135/pdf

Davey Anderson

Extract from *The Static*

'We all have sick thoughts. It doesnae matter what you think, it's what you do that counts. Trouble is, my thoughts do things. Don't believe me? Just watch.'

Sparky is a bright but volatile fifteen-year-old on the brink of permanent exclusion from school. Then one day he falls under the spell of a seemingly psychic girl called Siouxsie and develops his own kinetic superpower. *The Static* is a coming-of-age story about desire, guilt and mind over matter and was first performed in August 2012 at the Underbelly, Edinburgh. Cast:

Writer: Davey Anderson
Director and Choreographer: Neil Bettles
Lighting Designer: Simon Wilkinson
Creative Assistant: Jonnie Riordan

Setting: A high school in a small town on the West Coast of Scotland.

Characters:
SPARKY, a fifteen-year-old boy
SIOUXSIE, a fifteen-year-old girl
MRS KELLY, a woman in her thirties
MR MURPHY, a man in his late twenties

The performers double up as storytellers: B, S, P and N (based on the names of the original cast, Brian Vernel, Samantha Foley, Pauline Lockhart and Nick Rhys, respectively. Stage directions indicate where other, minor characters speak ('Teacher:' on p. 104, for example).

Scene Four

Sparky and Siouxsie are left alone in an empty classroom.
Sparky wears a giant pair of headphones.

SIOUXSIE What you listening to?

No response.

Hey, bawheid. I'm talking to you.

SPARKY What?

SIOUXSIE What are you listening to?

SPARKY Nothing.

SIOUXSIE Gies a shot.

SPARKY Nut.

SIOUXSIE Are they even plugged in?

No response.

N Siouxsie is cool as fuck.

P She spells her name S I O U X S I E. As in Siouxsie Sioux. As in Siouxsie and the Banshees.

N Never heard of them.

P The way Siouxsie tells it, if she had been born three hundred years ago, they would have burnt her at the stake.

Sparky looks at Siouxsie's thick black eyeliner, her black nail polish.

SPARKY   Whit you here for?

SIOUXSIE   Me? Pushed a girl down the stairs.

SPARKY   Did ye?

SIOUXSIE   Aye. Pushed her down the stairs without touching her.

Beat.

SPARKY   How'd you push somebody down the stairs without touching them?

Siouxsie's eyes twinkle.

N   Jesus Christ, she is gorgeous.

SIOUXSIE   Whit?

SPARKY   What?

SIOUXSIE   Did you say something?

SPARKY   Naw.

SIOUXSIE   You're weird.

SPARKY   So are you. How'd you push someone down the stairs?

SIOUXSIE   Easy. I just pictured it in my head. Like a hand coming out from inside my chest. Pushing. Boom! And down she went.

SPARKY   You mean she fell?

SIOUXSIE   Naw. I pushed her.

SPARKY   Without touching her?

SIOUXSIE   That's what I said.

SPARKY   You're full of shit.

SIOUXSIE   I've killed hundreds of people. Literally. Don't believe me?

SPARKY   Nut.

SIOUXSIE   Look at all the famous cases of poltergeists in history. What's
the one thing they all have in common?

SPARKY   I don't know.

SIOUXSIE   Guess.

SPARKY   Slime?

SIOUXSIE   Pubes. Tits. Periods.

Sparky blushes.

I'm telling ye. There's always, always, a teenage girl somewhere
nearby. You think that's a coincidence?

SPARKY   Maybe.

SIOUXSIE   The fuck it is. I could make your heartbeat stop dead if I wanted
to.

Sparky's heart skips a beat.

N   Fuck me. She is beautiful.

B   Shit! Did she hear that? I hope to God she didn't hear that.

SIOUXSIE   It's okay. There's no need to be embarrassed.

N   Can she hear me?

SIOUXSIE   Relax.

B   Oh my God. I think I'm gonnae be sick.

Teacher:

P   I can hear you two, muttering. Silence please, or you'll be here all lunchtime.

Siouxsie whispers in Sparky's ear.

SIOUXSIE   You going to Modern Studies after lunch?

SPARKY   Naw.

SIOUXSIE   Me neither. Meet you on the roof?

He nods.

N   And just like that Sparky is totally smitten.

Scene Five

On the roof.

N   Things you need to know about Siouxsie:
           When Siouxsie turned twelve, weird shit started happening to her.

P   Correction. When Siouxsie turned twelve, she started to make weird shit happen.

N   The time the school bus tipped over and everybody thought the driver was drunk? That was her.

P   The time the chimney fell off the roof and nearly killed her next-door neighbour? That was her.

SPARKY   Are you serious?

SIOUXSIE   Cross my heart and hope to die.

P   As soon as she hit puberty, that was it. It's like she developed an extra sense.

N   Or opened a door into another dimension.

SIOUXSIE   There's a boy in Iceland. His mum wanted him to go and live with his dad in London. The boy didn't want to go. So he looked up at the sky, pictured the bright blue turning dark and grey. Next day… ash cloud over Europe, every flight grounded.

SPARKY   Cool.

SIOUXSIE   There's a girl in Japan. She got bullied at school. So she went to the beach. Dared the sea to rise up and swallow her whole. A week later… Earthquake. Tidal wave. All her classmates got trapped in the school and drowned.

SPARKY   So who did you kill?

Siouxsie unzips her school bag.

SIOUXSIE   I'll show you.

She takes out a little book, full of scribbles, stuffed with photographs and scraps, bits and pieces of memorabilia. She leafs through the photos, searching for the right one.

            There.

She hands him the photograph.

SPARKY   Who's this? Is that you when you were a baby?

SIOUXSIE It's my sister. Step-sister.

Sparky realises.

SPARKY   Is this who you…?

Siouxsie nods solemnly.

          How did you kill her?

SIOUXSIE I wrote it in here.

SPARKY   What, in that wee book?

SIOUXSIE You ever heard of cosmic ordering?

He shakes his head.

          Didn't think so.

SPARKY   Is that like some kind of psychic online shopping?

SIOUXSIE All you have to do is write down what you want. Write it somewhere special. And if you really, really want it… it will happen.

SPARKY   Fuck off.

SIOUXSIE Fine. Don't believe me.

She snatches the photograph and carefully places it back into her book.

P   Do you want to hear the true story of how Siouxsie killed her sister?

Step-sister.

It goes something like this:

Siouxsie's dad is off the scene. One day, Siouxsie's mum comes home with a new boyfriend. A couple of weeks later, they get married. A few weeks after that, Siouxsie's mum starts to show.

S   Fucking bastard.

Step-dad:

N   You don't like me, do you?

No response.

Let's try to be friends. For your mother's sake.

No response.

You're going to have a new sister to play with.

S   'With God as my witness, that child will never grow old enough to call me sister.'

P   Before you know it, the bastard child is delivered through the front door.

Siouxsie peers into the cot, her nose turned up.

S   Ugly little creature, in't she?

N   Susan, go to your room.

Siouxsie takes out her book and writes the fateful sentence:

S   'May you breathe your last in the dark and never wake to see the light of day.'

P	She went to sleep that night with the book under her pillow, the bedroom window wide open.
N	She woke to the sound of her mother screaming, the baby blue in the face, cold and still.
P	And she just knew.
S	I did that. That was me.
P	That was the first time it happened. After that she couldn't help herself. Sinking cruise liners, toppling buildings.
N	She started wearing black 'cos she was in mourning.
P	She hasn't stopped.
N	Yet.

On the roof…
Siouxsie writes a new sentence.
Sparky watches her.

SPARKY   What you writing now?

SIOUXSIE You'll find out. If it comes true.

She stuffs the book into her schoolbag and zips it up.

In the corridor…
Sparky spies on Siouxsie as she places the schoolbag into her locker.

N	For the rest of the afternoon Sparky is in a daze. All he can think about is the mad glint in Siouxsie's eyes, the snarl on her lips, her sickly white skin.

David Yezzi

A Stop Before Starting

The only time I've been to Switzerland
was early one spring on a train through the mountains.
There was a lake – I guess it was Lucerne?
Above me cliff-tops ridged with snow fanned out
so that where I stood at the edge of the platform
light bathed the empty siding all around
with a diffused opalescence off the water.

Behind the station must have been a town,
spires of churches, municipal arcades,
and coffee squelching in the fogged cafés.
I never saw the place, though I remember
thinking this is Switzerland and took
a mind-shot of the pines, breathing-in the cold
as the porter whistled for us to reboard.

Pals

They don't mind the give-and-take:
the more you deke, the more they're jake.

The more you rage, the tougher they back you,
denouncing non-pals who attack you.

Pals are your mirror's true reflection.
They'll knock on doors for your election.

And pals pay back. No pal's too pure
to find his pal a sinecure.

If you have doubts, pals will ease them;
if guilty thoughts, let pals appease them.

A pal can lead you to the trough
or help you take a few pounds off

with just a word – it's merely fact –
and, failing that, pals manage tact.

It's for the best. That's all pals wish you.
They take your side on every issue.

Pals find means to fit your ends,
but how long they stay pals depends

on the ways you are simpatico.
How do they know? Pals know. They know.

Pan Am

ABC, Fall 2011

A torn TV poster
with five gleaming faces
and ten legs *passant*
in stewardess blue.

All feed hopes
for their new-fledged lives
(the actresses, too),
unaware that the plug

was yanked at the network
weeks ago due
to soft commitment
or busted luck.

Lack of belief
was not their failing.
Just look at this ad –
so coltish, so bluff.

Even so, it ended,
despite their ardour.
Our starred story,
recast in dreams,

of who we were then –
heralds of the busy air
and of long sky views –
slowly set down.

The Catches

I have a home   I don't like to go home to.
Stupid people have placed a ban   on stupid.

They've all slowed down to savour   things they missed.
What you wished for is pretty much   what happened.

She has amassed important   memories.
He fought so long   he lost the sense of fighting.

What revelations have come   have come too soon.
Despite large changes   nothing really happened.

I have no memory   of that conversation.
Inside the seed the full-grown flower   is wilting.

Finally we can see over   the falls.
My opposite is not   your opposite.

Of the five women   each one had her reasons.
The mathematician disproved   his own proof.

I love the stars   but can't name hardly any.
Let's say for instance   this is what we said.

Peter Arnott

Extract from *White Rose*

Based on fact and inspired by the book *Night Witches* by Bruce Myles, *White Rose* is the story of the brief career of Lily Litvak as a fighter pilot in the Red Army in 1942–43. It premiered at the Traverse Theatre on 22 May 1985, directed by Stephen Unwin.

Cast:
Kate Duchene as Lily
Tilda Swinton as Ina
Ken Stott as Alexei

Ina's Hands

Lily sits and reads a letter she has written.

LILY Dearest Mamoushka, I am writing this sitting in the cockpit in readiness. I'm thinking of sitting with you in our dear home. I am eating my favourite fritters in my dreams. I don't get at all cold, since you ask. In fact, flying at night is a bit like flying in a warm sock. You must keep reminding yourself what you're doing. I really feel part of the Yak now. It's like we've grown up together. Please remember to send father's photograph next time. Your loving daughter, Lily.

She folds the letter and settles to sleep. Ina comes in, her hands injured. She attempts to bandage them silently. But she moans, and Lily wakes.

LILY   Ina… what's the matter?

INA   Nothing, Lily. You go back to sleep.

LILY   Ina. Are you going to tell me what's wrong?

INA   I hurt my hands a little. That's all. Nothing to worry about.

Lily crosses to her and looks at her hands.

LILY   Let's have a look.
             [She sees that it's bad.]
             Oh, Ina!
             [She takes over the first aid.]
             So what happened?

INA   I left my gloves off. Some skin froze. Got stuck. And came off on the engine.

LILY   Oh… Ina!

INA   Look, don't bother… you need to rest.

LILY   It's no bother.
             [She treats Ina's hands in silence for a moment.]
             Why on earth did you take your gloves off?

INA   I was having an argument.

LILY   Were you having an argument, little Ina?

INA   I took my gloves off, and threw them on the ground to make a point.

LILY   And hurt your hands?

INA   Yes!

LILY   **[finishing]** There's my brave girl. Who were you having an argument with?

INA   One of your flight. Meklin.

LILY   What did he say? I'll sort him out for you.

INA   He wouldn't let me work on his aircraft. I mean, he wasn't doubting my ability or anything like that. He just didn't want me touching it. Like I had a disease or something.

LILY   How stupid of him.

INA   So I said to him, have I got the plague or something? Are you scared I'll put a curse on your engine, are you?

LILY   Well, Ina… a pilot does have the right to choose the engineers they want to work on their aircraft. After all, it's the pilot who has to fly the thing.

INA   That's what he said. Before he said I was getting hysterical.

LILY   You're tired, that's all.

INA   Don't be an idiot, Lily. Tell Meklin he's tired.

LILY   The men… will take time to adjust.

INA   Oh yes. Let's all be reasonable about it. It's fine for you. They've adjusted to you flying all right.

LILY   You know how long that took. You know the time I had.

INA   I know that I stood up for you. I supported you. But you will still not choose to stand for me against one of your precious bloody pilots. Because you're a pilot. And it is too much of me to ask you to show me some support… too much to expect a little solidarity.

LILY	I'm a pilot first, Ina. They all know that. I'm not married, I've got no children, so it doesn't make any difference.

INA	You're such a fool sometimes, Lily. You think you know when you're well off. But you don't know that you're insulted. When they insult me. And you pretend to yourself it isn't there.

LILY	What isn't there?

INA	You don't hear the things they say. The things I hear when I finish work and they're all drunk. And you didn't see the disgust in that little boy's eyes when he thought of my hands on his engine. You've forgotten what it's like. To hate yourself. The way men can make you hate yourself. Because you think you're just like them, don't you? One of the lads? Well, you're not. You're not. No matter how normal they pretend to be. You've started hating me now, haven't you? You're sitting there thinking what a bloody woman I am.

LILY	What do you want from me? A confession?

INA	I want you to support me. I want you on my side.

LILY	Do you want me to go on strike? Look… you should go and see the Women's Commissar at Division. This is her job. She'll tell you…

INA	She'll tell me what Lenin said. She'll tell me all about Lenin and Krupskaya and the partnership of men and women in revolutionary struggle.

LILY	I don't have time for this conversation.

INA   I bet you that's what Lenin said.

LILY   Look… there is bound to be residual prejudice…

INA   Residual prejudice! You know that doesn't sound too bad. I'm
             sure Meklin can cope with being a victim of anachronism. I'm
             sure he'll correct this tendency as soon as he has a spare moment.
             We all go to the same schools, everyone keeps telling us how
             equal we all are… all he has to do is understand it properly…

LILY   Settle down for God's sake. We haven't fought before, so why do
             you want to spoil things now?

INA   Oh, am I spoiling your war for you, Lily?… how selfish of me,
             just when it was going so well…

LILY   Don't be so stupid!

INA   Don't be such a stupid woman?

[pause]

LILY   We can't do this, Ina… we've got to settle…

INA   Settle for what?

LILY   For what there is! This isn't the place for this conversation, Ina.

INA   Where is the place for this conversation?

LILY   **[pause]** I'm sorry if you think I'm behaving like a man, if that
             is what I'm doing, but man woman or beast I've got to fly a
             mission with the rest of them in three hours' time. I'll be facing
             a squadron of Messerschmidts… with them… in three hours.
             I don't have time to think about it.

INA   Just try… for me… just try not to be so proud. That there is no time to think about it. That… is thinking like a man.

[pause]

LILY   How are your hands?

INA   They're alright.

[pause]

LILY   I'm sorry.

INA   That's all right. War brings out the best in people. I chose a bad moment for a crisis.

LILY   Well…

INA   What?

LILY   I had a bit of a crisis myself today.

INA   You did?

LILY   Why not? I'm entitled to a crisis too.

INA   I didn't say you weren't. Tell me.

LILY   Today… tonight… I was flying with Salomaten, and we passed a flight of Heinkels. We passed them. We let them go and bomb our men in the tractor factory. I broke radio silence to protest, and Alexei was furious. He said we'd get them on the way back when they were short of fuel. We got two of them. And it cost maybe a hundred… two hundred Russian lives. He fights so cynically, Ina. All he wants to do is shoot down Germans… like it's a game. He isn't fighting for his homeland or anything else.

That's his homeland, up there… shooting down Germans. I don't know, Ina. It scares me. It seems like… indiscipline. I think that we're fighting not to lose, Ina… not to be wiped out. I don't think I can think about it any further than that. I'm the trigger on a flying gun. I just fire where I'm pointed.

INA   Lily… are you in love with Alexei Salomaten?

LILY   Yes. Are you?

Assignation

Alexei drinks, and repeats words from a funeral oration he has given.

ALEXEI   Barnarov was my friend, as well as my commander. We fought in many a campaign together. Spain. That was the warm one. Finland, Moscow, Leningrad. All bitter. And now here. As an officer and as a man, his loss will be sorely felt.
[he stops quoting]
This war has gone and touched me. No. It has. And now I can hear the guns. All the time. Before, I could shut them out, most of the time, but now I'm listening to the guns. And, oh yes. I'm getting the message. You don't fool me, you clapped out old fraud. You're fucked. You're past it. On the slippery fucking slope for absolutely sure. Old Barnarov would have understood. When you've been in this business for a while, you come to recognise it in your comrades. This little distance behind the eyes. You're not all there. And there isn't long to go, when you slip into the sheets with death… and the bastard's still there in the morning. Killing people is just flirting with it. This. This is a wedding, when you're inviting your bullet… when You just don't care for just one second. That's enough. So, I will drink, to make this marriage more bearable, and I will make love to Lily Litvak. I will cheat on death. Loving Lily and killing Germans might conceal from me my thinness on this earth. I do hope it's nothing catching. Lily. I need you.

Lily enters.

LILY   You sent for me?

ALEXEI   Oh no. I hope I didn't send for you. I sent word I'd like to see you. There's a difference. Please. Sit down.

LILY   **[sitting]** Thank you, sir.

ALEXEI   Well, Lieutenant Litvak. How are things with you now?

LILY   Not so bad, thanks.

ALEXEI   You're pleased with your promotion?

LILY   Yes, sir. I'm just sorry…

ALEXEI   For what?

LILY   The circumstances.

ALEXEI   Well… that's how it is.

LILY   Yes, Sir.

ALEXEI   Good. So, you're feeling more settled in with us now. I can imagine what you've been through.

LILY   Can you, sir?

ALEXEI   Well, I hope so. I'd be a poor excuse for a flight leader…or a squadron commander… now… if I didn't notice these things.

LILY   Yes, sir. I'm sorry, sir.

ALEXEI   Yes. Well. Would you like a drink?

LILY   Oh. Yes, thank you.

ALEXEI [pouring two drinks] I couldn't have asked you that a few weeks ago, could I?

LILY   Couldn't you? Why not?

ALEXEI It would have been tactically unsound. But now that I've been informed that the Fourth Tank Corps have shaken hands with the Twenty Sixth, and that the enemy are now encircled, with no means of getting away, I didn't think that you would resist the urge to celebrate.

LILY   This has just happened?

ALEXEI Yes.

LILY   Then we must celebrate. What's the toast?

ALEXEI You choose.

LILY   [stands] Marshall Zhukov. Saviour of Moscow. Liberator of Stalingrad.

ALEXEI Here's to the old Cossack.
        [They drink, Alexei takes the glasses to refill them.]
        I would throw our glasses in the fireplace. But I've only got these… and I haven't got a fireplace.

He gives her her glass.

LILY   Your turn.

ALEXEI Oh. Very well.
        [He raises his glass.]
        To us. May we see the summer.

LILY   Yes. I suppose that's right. To us.

They drink. Alexei pours another.

ALEXEI Here. No toasts attached. This one is purely for purposes of leisure.

LILY   Shall I fetch Ina? I'm sure she'd like to celebrate as well.

ALEXEI No. Don't do that.

LILY   Why not?

ALEXEI You used to make me feel uncomfortable, you know. You used to scare the life out of me. You're a wonderful pilot. Everybody says so.

LILY   Do they?

ALEXEI Oh, yes. Everybody.

[pause]

LILY   Tell me about Barnarov. You and Barnarov.

ALEXEI You'd like that, would you?

LILY   He was your oldest friend. It's only natural to be upset. But if you don't want to talk about it…

ALEXEI You're very beautiful, Lily. That's no reflection on your abilities as a pilot, by the way.

LILY   Oh. Well. Thanks.

ALEXEI They made you cut your hair, didn't they?

LILY   It has to be practical. But some of the other girls have never cut
          their hair at all. And the men all like it. That annoys some of the
          rest of us, I can tell you.

ALEXEI   I imagine.

LILY   There's nothing inconsistent about caring how you look.

ALEXEI   Inconsistent with what?

LILY   Fighting. Killing fascists. So long as it doesn't interfere.

ALEXEI   Well, there's no looking good by accident. Besides, it makes you
          accessible. Makes you a good comrade.

LILY   Am I a good comrade?

ALEXEI   Yes. Have another drink.

LILY   No, really. It concerns me.

ALEXEI   What can I tell you? Who's telling you you're not...

LILY   Well…

ALEXEI   People of your generation continually astound me. You are all so
          serious.

LILY   Our situation is serious.

ALEXEI   Yes. We know that. We know that. So you don't need to continually
          demonstrate it. All right? It's a waste of energy, and it's bad for
          morale. Hang the sense of it and fly. Just fly, damn it. Flying is
          what we are good at. Leave the ideology to the ideologists. That's
          what they're good at, Lily. Serious people are serious because they
          enjoy it, in my experience. And good luck to them. Not me. Not

everyone can be a philosopher, which is obvious to everyone except philosophers. Be honest with yourself. You know what matters to you. And to me. And it's up there, Lily. You are a pilot, yes? Well I am a soldier, and all soldiers are the same deep down. Thick as pig shit and grateful for it. Oh, we can deploy a smattering of Marxese whenever we might need it, but we have to concentrate on doing our job. Which is not a job for philosophers. It's a job for professionals. We are here to kill Germans. The rest is decoration. Cheers.

He drinks and pours another.

LILY   Don't you think there will be Germans fighting for Hitler who think exactly the same way?

ALEXEI 'Course there are. I've trained with them. Back in 1940. Why?

LILY   Doesn't that worry you?

ALEXEI No. I don't think so. If you're asking me whether I think I've got more in common with a Luftwaffe pilot than I do with a commissar, yes, I should think I probably have. Monstrous, of course. But as long as the philosophers insist on proving their philosophies in wars, they'll just have to put up with ignorant barbarians like you and me fighting their wars for them.

LILY   I believe in what I'm fighting for.

ALEXEI I know. You're anomalous and you upset me. Because you are a real pilot and a real philosopher… all at the same time. It's people like you, pioneers like you, who have made it possible for clods like me to fly at all. You're an original. Bleriot, Lindbergh, Raskova… Litvak. Well..it sounds a little Jewish, possibly…

LILY   My grandfather was Jewish.

ALEXEI You mustn't pander to egalitarianism, Lily. It ill becomes angels to be democratic. And be honest with me. You don't believe that you're 'just another pilot' any more than I do.

LILY   You're impossible.

ALEXEI   Drunk. Don't confuse excess with originality...

LILY   Ina says…

ALEXEI   Oh… Ina! Ina is an engineer. The salt of the earth, no doubt. But you are a flier. Lily Litvak is a flier first and last. It is different for you. You know it is. So don't worry about Ina, don't worry about anything, just…

LILY   Fly.

ALEXEI   Fly.

He goes to pour another drink.

LILY   Don't drink any more.

ALEXEI   Just you try and stop me.

She kisses him. They look at each other.

ALEXEI   How old are you, Litvak?

LILY   I'm very young.

They kiss again.

ALEXEI   I'm a worn out old heretic, Lily. You're going to have to accept that.

LILY   Nothing's changed, Alexei.

ALEXEI   Hasn't it?

LILY   No. There's no reason for us not to be lovers, as long as it fits in
            with killing as many Germans as possible. We must be sure we're
            consistent in what we're doing.

ALEXEI   Well, that's right.

LILY   I feel very positive about it.

ALEXEI   Yes?

LILY   Hmn. Very confident.

ALEXEI   Good.

LILY   I've got to get back. Come to my quarters tomorrow night. We
            won't talk on the field in the morning. We've got to be careful. We
            can't lose strength in love. It's got to be part of our strength. We
            mustn't see each other as a retreat from the struggle.

ALEXEI   No, of course not.

LILY   Let's just concentrate on getting down safely and finding
            somewhere to make love. I'll check Ina's duty rosta.

ALEXEI   All right.

LILY   Good night then.

ALEXEI   Good night.

Lily exits. Alexei pours another drink and drains it.

ALEXEI   Girl scouts. Junior bloody girl scouts. What do you think,
            Barnarov? 'We mustn't see each other as a retreat from the
            struggle'. I am wet from the smell of you, Litvak. And I can't hear
            the guns at all.

Fiona Wilson

Velvet Jacket

A wersh, dry wind off the Forth
brings him hirpling up Heriot,
all shoulders, elbows, joints,
hair too black, too lank, 'doggedly
debonair', the urchins' chants
('ya yallow yite!') fluttering
after, scarf-like in the air –

which tends to a snap and a flicker
in the New Town's angled plot.
Now, Circles, Rows, and perfect Squares,
those 'draughty parallelograms', are tipping,
twirling, slipping downhill, into a blurred
and sketchy escape. An infantine blue
is the old sea road, the known way forth from the Forth.

Cramasie

I went down to How-D'ye-Do,
its crowded streets and tripper tourists,
its songbird market, and hullabaloo
and I wore cramasie, cramasie, cramasie –

I went down to Devil-May-Care,
its wind-up toys and plastic frippery,
its gee-gee races and 'business affairs'
and I wore cramasie, cramasie, cramasie –

I went down to The-Buck-Stops-Here.
It was lonely there, the crowds gone home.
Steel shutters banged, I couldn't stop there,
though I wore cramasie, cramasie, cramasie –

Wonders Will Never Cease

A bird I've never seen before
bleeds across my sight:
a Cardinal I'll learn it is, that
or rarer, a Scarlet Tanager –

Not I'll admit that those
are my first thoughts:
more like ferlie or freak,
la-di-gagging-grandiose.

Something released or
escaped? The tame
in the wild run wild?
Stranger this will be, and stranger –

An Italicised 'O'

Not the ambush up 'the lane', not the fist in the stomach, the assisted slump, not the shoe, the chute, the –

oh, much worse, I did it myself, mixed grit and flesh, a hole in my green wool tights, and dear-dear-dear, somebody's-been-in-the-wars,

and now, to cap it all, my rounding wail –
'I fell… I fell… I fell.'

Nicola McCartney

Extract from *Lifeboat*

Lifeboat is the extraordinary true story of Bess Walder and Beth Cummings. It is a story of courage, a story of survival, a story of enduring friendship. On Friday 13 September 1940, *The City of Benares* set sail from Liverpool for Canada. On board were ninety evacuees escaping the relentless bombing and dangers of war torn Britain. Four days into the crossing, the ship was torpedoed and sank. Only eleven of the evacuees survived. Two fifteen-year-old girls, Bess Walder and Beth Cumming, spent nineteen terrifying hours in the water on an upturned lifeboat. They willed each other to survive. They remained firm friends for the rest of their lives.

Lifeboat won the TMA/Equity Award for Best Production for Children and Young People in 2002 and has toured and been reproduced all over the world since.

Lifeboat was first produced by Catherine Wheels Theatre Company at the Brunton Theatre, Musselburgh, in 2002.

Director: Gill Robertson
Designer: Karen Tennent
Composer: Dave Trouton
Lighting Designer: Jeanine Davies
Cast: Suzanne Robertson and Gemma Burns

Characters:
Bess Walder   15
Beth Cummings   14

Setting: a lifeboat adrift in the North Atlantic, 1940.
The ship rocks about more violently, throwing them all over the place.
BESS is seasick.

BETH   Are you all right…? We'd better get downstairs.

BESS   Hang on.

BETH   What for…? What's wrong? Bess?

BESS   The Navy… Where have the other ships gone ?

BETH   I don't know… They've.

BESS   Vanished.

BESS   Grey everywhere as far as the eye can see.

BETH   Dark, but it's only six o'clock

BESS   All's not well.

BETH   It's only six o'clock and they put us to bed…

BESS   With no tea.

BETH   Down the wooden hill to Bedfordshire.

BESS   Sleep.

BETH   I can't sleep.

BESS   Go to sleep.

They sleep.
Time passes.

Sound of a torpedo approaching.
An explosion and the ship rocks violently
The girls are thrown out of bed. A bell rings.

BESS   The first thing was the bang – a bang bigger than any I'd heard in the blitz.

BETH   An explosion. A smell of burning.

BESS   Burning chocolate, burning oil, burning…

BETH   Fire! We're on fire!

BESS   We had to get out.

BETH   I looked at the other girls in my cabin. We knew what had happened – a torpedo. The Gerries had got us.

BESS   Me and the other girls in my cabin, Alice and Dora, leapt out of bed.

BETH   The ships rocked and the big heavy wardrobe came falling towards me.

BESS   The wardrobe just missed my legs, but it fell right on top of Alice. She couldn't move. Me and Dora tried to lift the wardrobe but it was too heavy.

BETH   My leg was hurt, it was bleeding. I could hardly walk.

BESS   Alice was trapped.

BETH   We did what we'd practised in the drill – put on our lifejackets and get to the rocking horse muster station. The adults were very strict with us – we were not allowed to panic. We were not allowed to run.

BESS   We made lots of noise, banging on the doors of the wardrobe. An officer came with an axe and chopped through the door. We had to climb over the top of the wardrobe and out of the door. But Alice was still trapped underneath it. We wanted to help her, but one of the escorts told us to get above decks, so we did. She told us Alice would be alright. We had to leave her behind.

Bess and Beth make their way through the debris of the ship that is collapsing around them, up onto the deck.

BETH   One of the escorts picked me up because I couldn't walk and carried me upstairs to the deck.

BESS   The water was up to our ankles – the ship was sinking fast. We tried to go up the usual staircase but it had collapsed. We had to find another way out. I could see through the floor – there were big gaps everywhere and you could look right down down down into the decks below.

BETH   On the deck it was pitch black. The only light was from the fireworks, I think they're called flares, which the sailors were setting off to let people know we were in trouble. The sky was all red and yellow like on bonfire night. It was really pretty.

BESS   A sailor shoved me up a broken staircase and another one lifted me onto the deck.

BETH   A man lifted me into a lifeboat. BESS A man lifted me into a lifeboat.

BESS   I was looking for Lou.

BETH   They started to lower the lifeboat into the sea.

BESS   I was looking for my brother.

BETH   I was thinking, we're going to be safe now.

BESS   Then

BETH   The end of the lifeboat – my end started dipping.

BESS   We were going down at an angle, heading into the sea.

BETH   I looked up. Above us the ropes were entangled. A sailor took a knife and cut the ropes and we

BESS   Plunged into the ocean…

BETH   It was alright… we were floating.

BESS   But then

BETH   The lifeboat's filling up with…

BESS   Water.

BETH   Water? [In pain.] Salt hurts. My leg hurts.

BESS   Water. Up to my knees.

BETH   I say to the little children beside me, 'Keep your heads up.'

BESS   Up to my waist…

BETH   The little ones are drowning.

BESS   Up to my chest…

BETH   Up, up, up. Keep your heads up.

BESS   They're drowning.

[pause]

BETH   Oh no.

BESS   Don't think about it.

BESS   The lifeboat's sinking. Water up

BETH   To my neck.

BETH   To my chin.

BESS   Deep breath!

Beth and Bess both take a huge breath.
The lifeboat capsizes.
They are under the water.

BESS   Down... Cold and dark and... And... And... Lost my pyjama
        bottoms... Nearly lost my... Glasses... My glasses... Drowning...
        No... Not drowning...

BETH   Down... Like a lift out of control, like a big Ferris wheel, too
        fast... I can't swim, what do I do? I can't swim... Too fast... going
        to hit the... No... Got to...

BESS   Remember what Dad said... Remember...

DAD   Remember, Young Woman. Here's the thing about diving. A human
        being is like a cork – it floats. When you go under... Relax... Let
        your arms go... Wide... Float... That's it... No point kicking. Save
        your strength... That's it... When you come up... That's when the
        work really starts... Now kick...

She swims to the surface and breaks through.

BESS   I made it!   BETH   I made it!

BESS   I grabbed hold of the upturned lifeboat.

BETH   And I grabbed hold of the lifeboat

BESS   And we stayed there all night.

Bess and Beth cling to the lifeboat. The sun rises.

BESS   Beth…?

BETH   Mm-hmmm?

BESS   I think I might be nearly dead.

BETH   Me too.

BESS   Should we just let go?

First, Beth sees giant fish jumping in and out of the water. Then Bess sees huge trays of food being carried by silver turbans. Lastly, they see the rocking horse and imagine themselves flying on it – perhaps they sing, or just have the music of 'Don't fence me in' again at this point. Then the voices of the HMS *Hurricane* men gradually cut in over it, drawing us back to reality.

VOICES Hello… Hello… It's children… How many?… One, two, maybe three… Hang on, we're coming.

Ben Wilkinson

Stag

The one I saw on the bypass that summer night –
antlers like a winter oak's branches
as it strode from the roadside –
came again in a dream; warily keeping
its distance as it does each and every time.

When I met it for real I kept mine:
shocked by its presence
on a road without so much as headlights;
its still and eerie silhouette
held there before it turned and left.

In the dream, though, I cut loose and follow –
into fields and blackening meadows
where it spots me, begins to trot,
then picks up pace before galloping off.
So what if I could get close enough,

look it in those cavernous eyes,
the moon backlighting a shimmering hide?
What else could I hope to find
except all you said surface in my mind
as its glare passes right the way through me?

Knowledge

Watching these white-black birds in flight –
ink-dipped wings scribbling patterns
over water and sky –

I think of that naturalist,
hard at work,
penning his lofty treatise *On Birds*:

their summer absence
from the Solway Firth
given their birth from barnacles;

how they might take flight –
or hopelessly fall –
from the boughs of a fabled tree;

or how, through
the otherwise lean days of Lent,
they were eaten by members of the clergy

while the birds, of course,
simply swoop and bark among themselves –
waves crashing into the pier –

same as they've always done,
same as they always will;
rewriting the skyline, until they disappear.

Hound

When it comes, and I know how it comes
from nowhere, out of night like some
shadow falling on streets, how it waits
by the door in such steady silence –
a single black thought, its empty face –

don't let it tie you down to the house,
don't let it slope upstairs to spend
long hours coiled next to your bed,
but force the thing out, make it trudge
for miles in cold and wind and sleet.

Have it follow you, the faithful pet
it pretends to be, this awful mutt
like a heavy, half-arsed Cerberus,
tell it where to get off when it hangs
on with its coaxing, mournful look,

leave it tethered to some lamppost
and dismiss those pangs of guilt.
Know it's no dog there but a phantom,
its fur so dark it gives back nothing,
see how your hand passes through

its come-and-go presence, that air
of self-satisfied deception, just as
the future bursts in on the present,
its big *I am*, and that hulking hound –
sulking, whining – goes to ground again.

A Late Aubade

How long since we last lolled here all morning,
the house quiet and still, the snow falling
beyond our bedroom's window and warmth?
Now that we've time to uncover each other
after what seems like months apart –
losing ourselves in that same tender art
to open one thought onto another –
even this grim half-light has a charm of sorts.

Times like these grant us leave from the world –
those claims it makes of everyone –
and the constant doing that comes to nothing;
the snow still falls and the streets are frozen.
Instead, let this moment be perfectly held –
return us to something we hadn't thought missing.

David Greig

Extract from *Caledonia Dreaming*

Caledonia Dreaming (An Edinburgh Fantasy) was made in rehearsal during May 1997. Its characters, stories and ideas were created in collaboration with the 7:84 company.

Cast:

STUART	A Member of the European Parliament
LAUREN	A sauna worker
EPPIE	A woman from the Braids
DARREN	A boy from Oxgangs
JERRY	A doorman at the Caledonian Hotel
LAWRENCE	A taxi driver

Setting: A summer night in Edinburgh on the eve of devolution and Sean Connery is reported to be coming to stay at the Caledonian Hotel. Six Edinburgh residents have different reasons to try and find him. Darren, an unemployed boy from Oxgangs dreams of being Connery's PA and escaping from his dead-end life. Eppie, a hopelessly bored middle-class woman, reminisces about her youthful fling with Connery at Portobello outdoor swimming pool. Jerry, a doorman at the hotel who yearns to be a lounge crooner wants to slip his demo tape under Connery's door. Stuart, the local MEP, dreams of Connery's support in his boosterist plan to bring the Olympics to Edinburgh and he recruits the English sauna girl – Lauren – to help him succeed in his plan. The play winds through the course of one night following the characters' dreams of escape and rescue, culminating in a brief encounter with a long black limousine outside St Giles Cathedral. Throughout the play are wound 'choruses' which reflect on the devolutionary issues of the time the play was written.

40.

The Heart of Midlothian
Jakies drinking.

Excuse me.

Have you got a fag I could borrow?

All right. Cheers pal.

Have a good night.

[spit]

Why do people spit on the Heart of Midlothian?

Not football. And not Walter Scott.

And not because people in this town are dirty people.

No.

They spit because for other reasons.

They spit to remember the Edinburgh Mob. In 1736.

Which, fair enough, was a long time ago.

The people of Edinburgh had a riot.

Because a bunch of Bankers had sold their government.

The mob ran down the Cowgate.

And they ran up the High Street.

Cursing in an eighteenth century way.

Fie upon thee.

Zounds. And Pox on't.

They shouted and they hurled furniture down on the heads of British soldiers.

Then it was quite poor furniture.

But now it would be antique. And worth quite a lot of money.

The Mob rioted in 1780 and again in 1811 and even again in 1837. But for some time now, apart from a wee riot in Wester Hailes 1993, the Edinburgh mob have rioted only in their private lives. And the Edinburgh bankers have breathed easily.

Making money off people.

Forming governments to help them make money off people.

Cooking up schemes to make even more money off people.

Famed the world over for...

Stashing that cash.

Keeping a tight hold of those wads.

Oh they're canny little bankers.

And they breathe easily.

We don't riot now.

Maybe we should.

Instead we gob.

In the heart of the city.

In front of the courts.

In front of the cathedral.

Edinburgh folk pass by and have a quiet gob.

And you'll notice that when they do, they smile as if they'd just turned over a Porsche.

Because every gobbet of saliva that lands on this sacred heart is a little personal riot.

A warning to Bankers everywhere.

Available to all free citizens.

The world over.

Wherever you live.

Wherever you were born.

We're still here.

We're the Edinburgh mob

Have you got a fag on you, pal?

Cheers.

Have a good night.

[spit]

Fucking Bankers.

41.

Jerry in the cab.

JERRY   I don't know where I'm going yet. I'm looking for someone. She can't be far away.

        ...

Oh god.

…
Hello again.
What a coincidence,
Are you… feeling a bit better?
Good.
A decision.
Good.
In a time of crisis a decision's what you need.
Absolutely…
I'm looking for a woman.
Blonde.
No…
I like her but…
I hardly know her.
Tranquil… yes.
I feel sort of tranquil too.
Yes…
It feels OK to be tranquil.
Keep looking.
That's it… we'll just drive slowly around.
Yeah.
Slowly this time.
Good.
A poem… that's nice.
I'd love to hear it but…
Maybe you should keep your eyes on the road.
I'll read it.
OK OK

The taxi driver gives Jerry a piece of paper.

42.

Stuart is following Lauren up the High Street.

LAUREN Will you stop following me?

I'll call the police.

STUART   I can give you Bermuda.
         I'm offering you Florida.
         Oiling yourself on a beach.
         A tan.
         You're so pale. You need sunshine.

LAUREN   You're drunk.
         Go home.

STUART   You're a whore. She's a whore.
         Here.
         Cash.
         It's yours. You've only to pick it up.

He throws some money down on the Heart of Midlothian.

LAUREN   I don't want your money.

STUART   Please.

LAUREN   No.

STUART   Why not? What do you want?
         Don't tell me you want this.
         When I can give you St Tropez.
         When I am offering you London.
         Don't tell me you look around you at this life of piss you have and
         actually want it?

LAUREN   You're shouting.
         People are looking at you.

STUART   I'm shouting.
         (I'm shouting)

Yes I'm drunk but I don't understand.
I'm clever.
If I'm clever I should be able to understand.

LAUREN You want to know what I want?

STUART Name it. It's yours.

LAUREN I want to get married.
Have a kid.
Settle down in a nice house.
Maybe in Musselburgh, because it's almost the country, isn't it, and it's near the beach.
Maybe have neighbours.
Maybe do a wee job.

STUART I can give you that.

LAUREN No you can't.

STUART You're a beautiful woman.
You could be my secretary.
You could be my wife.

LAUREN No.

STUART I can pay.
I can have you if I want.
You cost fifty quid.

LAUREN If you don't leave me alone I'll put your name in the papers.

STUART I know what you want.
You want to spoil.
I've seen your type before.
You see a man's dreams and you want to piss on them.

This is what Scottish women are.

They're spoilers.

That's what's held us back.

LAUREN I'm English.

STUART Proves my point.

LAUREN Please go away.

STUART I am drunk.

Yes.

Sad. Yes. The suit, this is Armani by the way, is stained.

But I have strength.

I'm not afraid of you.

Please say yes to me.

I know that I can drag this country up behind me.

Even if it kicks and screams.

This will be an Olympic city.

This will be a place in the world.

LAUREN You're sitting in spit.

Your suit will have spit stains on it.

Jerry in the cab.

JERRY *The Knowledge* by Lawrence Chetty.

Do you want me to read it any particular way?

No. OK.

I have done the Edinburgh knowledge.

I remember all the streets.

And how to get from one.

To another.

I have done the knowledge

So why do I feel like

I don't know

Anything.
Anymore.
…
Woah…
Did I read it all right for you?
You should give writing a go.
You're quite a wordsmith.

Eppie and Darren arrive.

EPPIE Spit.

DARREN No.

EPPIE You'll enjoy it.

DARREN No.

EPPIE Don't sulk.
Shoulders back.
Anger, Darren. Gather up your anger.
Gather up a great big gob and spit.
I assure you.
It's therapeutic.

She spits.

DARREN There's a man there.

EPPIE Ignore him.

DARREN Maybe he's in trouble.
Sir? Have you dropped some money.

STUART A mugger. Now I'm mugged!
Take the money.

I don't want the fucking money.

DARREN   I don't want your money.

STUART   See! Even the muggers in this city have no ambition.

DARREN   Is he with you?

LAUREN   No.

DARREN   He's crying.
He's wearing a suit but he's crying.

EPPIE   That's the bloody trouble with this country.
Get out of the way, you smelly man.
We weep when we should be spitting.
Stand up.
Have some backbone.

She lifts up Stuart and slaps him.

STUART   You again. Christ. What are you – my mum?

EPPIE   Somebody ought to be.

Darren spits.
Lauren takes out a cigarette.
Darren goes to light it.

LAUREN   Thank you.

DARREN   I can only apologise for spitting in front of you.
It's a tradition.
It's something we locals do.

EPPIE   Have a gob, love.

It's good for the soul.
Brandy?

She offers all a nip of brandy.

STUART   Thank you.

DARREN Where are you from?

LAUREN I'm English.

DARREN Ahhh. I could tell from the accent.

LAUREN Have you got a problem with that?

DARREN Far from it.
I've never been to England.
But obviously I've seen it on the television, it seems quite OK.

LAUREN It is.

DARREN Rolling hills.
Green trees.
Little villages.
I'd like to visit one day.

LAUREN What's your name?

STUART   Have you ever seen the sky change colour, Missis?

EPPIE   It depends how many brandies I've had.
Sometimes the sky doesn't just change colour.
It spins around as well.

DARREN The name's Boyd. Darren Boyd.

LAUREN I'm Lauren.

STUART Imagine the sky rolling back.
The darkness actually sliding away and bright sunshine pouring
down on to us.
I have seen that.
That's something I've seen.

EPPIE Are you some kind of holy man?

STUART I am a visionary, missis.
I see visions.

EPPIE I always want to seduce religious types.
Just to see the shame on their faces.
More?

STUART Yes please.

DARREN Lauren. That's an enchanting name.
It's enjoyable just to say it.
Lauren.
You're lucky to be blessed with a name like that.

LAUREN Actually my name's Erica but Lauren is my work name.

DARREN You're an actress?

LAUREN Sort of.

DARREN I'm going to act, one day.
Of course you're probably already a pro.

LAUREN Darren.
Do you need any money?
Because that money there belongs to me.

And I don't want it.
You could buy yourself a new jacket.

DARREN What's wrong with my jacket?

LAUREN Nothing.

DARREN This is handmade.

LAUREN It's there if you want it.

DARREN This jacket has had only one previous owner.
It's got quality written all over it.
Are you sure you don't want the money?
It's quite a lot.

LAUREN You have it, Darren.

DARREN Maybe I'll keep it for you.
So that nobody steals it.
[He picks the money up.]
This is quite a lot… Here.

She gives him a polythene bag. He puts the money in it.

LAUREN I'm going to spit.

EPPIE Go on girl.
Get it out of you.

LAUREN Do you think of anything in particular, or do you just spit?

EPPIE Everything you hate, you visualise it.
And then you spit.

Silence. Lauren spits.

DARREN What did you think of?

LAUREN Him.

STUART I want to marry her.
But she doesn't want my money.

A taxi pulls up.
Jerry gets out.

JERRY Cheers mate, thanks…
No keep it…
Keep it… I insist.
OK.
Goodnight.
Remember…
You've got to have a dream!
If you don't have a dream!
How you gonna make a dream come true!
Yeah!
Thanks again.
Cheers.

EPPIE Have you come to spit?
It seems the entire city's come to expectorate.
We'll drown the buggers in a flood of phlegm.

JERRY No. I'm here for Lauren.

EPPIE She's called Lauren.

DARREN But it's only her professional name.
Her real name is Erica.

STUART I love her.
She understands me.

JERRY   Lauren…
Now I'm embarrassed. I…

DARREN Is this man bothering you?

LAUREN No. No he's a friend.

JERRY   A friend. Yes… but a tape…
No?
Did we have a moment?
I can't say… what I…
You. Here. Me. Tongue tied.
I mean…
Did we have a connection or was I dreaming?
All the clichés.
All the… look, stars!
And you said a drink…
but…
and…
'Take the ribbon from your hair.
Shake it loose and let it fall.
Laying soft against your skin.
Like the shadows on the wall.'
Gladys Knight and the Pips.

STUART Kris Kristofferson.

JERRY   I don't know any other way to say it.
You're right Lauren.
I want to be something I'm not.
But you see. I sing what I feel.
And you liked it.
So maybe I am what I'm not.
Maybe.
D'you understand?

LAUREN Yes.

EPPIE I am a woman who turned down a man once.
Because I thought he was tongue tied.

DARREN She regrets it.

EPPIE I regret it.
Thinking of it makes me want to spit.
But I won't.
That man's singing made my mouth dry.

STUART It gave me the dry boak.

JERRY What do you say, Lauren?

LAUREN You haven't asked a question for me to answer.

JERRY Will you…
I mean can we…
A drink… have…

He is about to sing again.

LAUREN No, don't sing.
The answer's yes.
Whatever.
I'll imagine the question.

DARREN Oh. Oh. Oh. Oh.

EPPIE He's hyperventilating.

DARREN Look! Look!

They turn and look.

Peter Mackay

Odysseus

You do not trust me to return to Ithaca,
the withered plants, tumbledown walls, lean-tos,
that will not weather an eleventh winter;

you doubt me an Achilles, after all,
try to remember a tender heel among my grumbles,
a slight limp on my left.

Was I arrogant enough to think myself a God?
How far – precisely –
did my interest in young men go?

I wish I could reassure you. But all I know
is one day I will doubt this island
Ithaca, and the next, and set off

home, not home, not home, home.

Gu leòr

Am bu dùraig dhomh an àradh ghabhail
sios dhan tearr agus dìosal,
mo chasan a chall san dorchadas,
gus uachdar an dubh-òl a bhruilleachadh
an uisge 's nan creataichean a ruaimleachadh
gus fhaicinn dè thigeas on doimhne –
Haig's Pinch, King's Ransom, Spey Royal,
Mountain Dew agus Old Curio,
3 millean nota Iamaicanach gun luach,
cotan, tombaca 's anainn –
air neo b' fheàrr, ann an gaothan a' Ghearrain,
na curtairean a tharraing ri taobh an teine
fo chomhair tuinn ag at 's sgàineadh air sgeirean
fo chomhair a' chionniceir a' cnead 's a' cnàmhan?

Enough

Do I dare go down the ladder
down into the diesel and tar,
lose my foothold out in the dark,
as I probe the black surface of oil,
stir the waters, the caskets and crates
to see what will spill from the deep –
Haig's Pinch, King's Ransom, Spey Royal,
Mountain Dew and Old Curio,
3 million priceless Jamaican pounds,
cotton, pineapple, tobacco –
or is it better in February's winds,
to draw the curtains beside the fire
on waves swelling and bursting on skerries
on the subterrane's clinking and groans?

Sionnachan

Chaidh proghan fodair fhàgail san fheur-lobht
fad iomadh bliadhna agus an taigh falamh:
sloc leth òrach leth thùngaidh far a shruthadh
a' ghrian mar shionnachan tro na cochaill
ga mùchadh fhèin air na leacan fuara.

Chrochamaid dealbhan reubte à irisean
air na sailthean, agus steigearan
on Album Phanini airson Mexico '86:
Burruchaga, Socrates 's Schumacher ri taobh
corrain trèigte, iarainn 's sàibh.

Chuireadh Alasdair lighter ris a' chonnlach
agus *marsinleibh* ghabhadh sopan ris,
diabhalan dearg-shùileach a' priobadh air.
Mar itealagan thuiteadh iad dhan làr
òr a' tionndadh gu luaithrean san adhar.

Will-o'-the-wisp

Dregs of fodder were left in the hayloft
for years, with the house lying empty:
a half-gold half-dank pit where the sun
skipped like will-o'-the-wisps through the husks
and was smothered on the slabs below.

We'd hang pictures ripped from magazines
on the joists, and stickers collected
from the Pannini Album for Mexico '86:
Ruggeri, Zico and Rummenigge jostling
the abandoned saw, scythe-blade and sickle.

Alasdair would put a lighter to the straw
and *jusslikethat* it would catch.
Red eyed devils would prick on,
madcap kites tumble to the ground
gold turn to ash in the air.

Utopia

Let me tell you something.
Lift my head down from this spike,
unboil it, flesh it out if you can,
bellow me to return the saintly pallor
to my cheeks, and I'll speak
to you of my visions of heaven
as far as it is in my power.

I will bring simple truth and order
to your thoughts, an idea of rhythm
that will act as God's mirror.
Most important: there is no freedom. If needed
we can mark this on your skin.
I keep a pot of quicksilver,
lead, a scarring tool, readied.

Heaven, though of the soul, is full-blooded
cut through with binding wire and deep hooks:
it is a land of the dead or half-dead,
approached, after all, in pain and letting
not through prayer or German books.
Strap a nubbed bridle tight to the head;
open veins to drop the lead in.

I'd have you remember me, the grace of dying,
how one man holds up the march of kings
how commonwealths are above all religious domains
how undue tolerance is a crime.
I, who feel the raven's kiss,
hear the tower's daily dirn:
remember me, I will be a boon to your time.

Joyce McMillan

The Traverse and Scotland

It's an observable fact about Scotland and its culture, that during all 306 years so far of the country's formal union with England it has remained both stubbornly present and oddly – not to say subtly – diminished. On one hand, the idea of Scotland and Scottishness has never looked like disappearing, not even at the time when serious efforts were made to have the whole place redefined, for postal purposes, as 'North Britain'. Yet on the other hand, for much of those three centuries, the UK's dominant London-based culture has sought to frame Scotland in one of a few subtly reductive ways, as a place or nation not complete in itself, but rather, adding an extra dimension to the metropolitan norm.

The stereotypes thrown up in this process are still familiar today, and provide a great deal of work for Scottish actors in London. There is the Highlander stereotype – popular not only in the south but in America – which frames Scotland as a remote place of bens and glens, shooting estates, loyal ghillies and rugged clansmen. There are a clutch of stereotypes more closely linked to the impact of Lowland Scots on British institutions over the years; the now largely defunct idea of Scots as well-educated, canny, ambitious, careful with money, and fond of a bit of sound engineering.

And then finally there is the 'hard man' stereotype, in which urban Scots typically appear as violent criminals – or occasionally policemen – with a drink problem, or a history of involvement with drugs. This image is partly a legacy – shared with parts of northern England – of Scotland's heavy industrial past, and the working-class culture it spawned. Yet it's also a reflection of a deeply rooted southern English belief, visible as far back as Shakespeare, that

Scotland must be a less civilised place than England; if it's grim up north, the argument seems to run, then it must be even more dangerous and barbaric once you pass Hadrian's Wall.

Now of course it's possible for any person actually living in modern Scotland to send these stereotypes up, to have a laugh at them, and to dismiss them as nonsense, irrelevant to contemporary Scottish life. Yet given their pervasive presence in the culture that dominates UK media, Scots still tend to internalise them, all the same. And what they all say, in differing tones of voice, is that Scotland belongs to the past, rather than the future; the past of Highland clan culture and the *White Heather Club*, the past of empire and the skills needed to run it, or the past of heavy industry and unreconstructed masculinity. London, New York and other world cities are full of talented Scots of a certain age who walked out of one of those narratives to become citizens of the modern world, and who see the leaving of Scotland as an essential part of their shift to modernity. Occasionally, they will return to the old country – frozen like Brigadoon in their memories – and harangue it about the need for change. Yet in truth, the Scotland they address is no longer there; because Scotland, too, has moved on, unbeknown to them, and sometimes also – because of the difficulties a stateless nation experiences in mediating itself to itself – unbeknown to itself.

And it's against this cultural background that the work of Scottish creative artists over the last two generations becomes so vitally important, as a sign of political change and a catalyst for it; not in any direct or obvious way, but in the mere fact of the presence of a powerful creative voice that comes from Scotland, and remains rooted here, but which concerns itself primarily with the present and the future of the global society in which we live. Given the fragile position of professional theatre in Scottish public life – long pushed to the margins after the Reformation, and most often associated, after its return, with visiting London companies – it may be easier to trace the impact on Scotland's cultural confidence of art-forms like music and literature; the huge Scottish rock music boom of the 1980s, and the coming of the generation of writers led by Alasdair Gray, Liz Lochhead, Iain Banks, Ian Rankin, A.L. Kennedy, Jackie Kay, Irvine Welsh and a dozen others, must have transformed the views of tens of thousands, in Scotland and beyond, about what 21st century Scotland is, and could be.

Yet it seems to me, from my own experience, that Scottish theatre has been intimately connected with that same movement towards the development of a distinctive, post-modern Scottish voice, emerging onto the world stage as we move into the new millennium. And if one theatre has been at the centre of that change, it has been the Traverse, the theatre that dedicates itself to producing new work, mainly by Scottish-based playwrights. The Traverse has played many other roles, of course, over the past fifty years. It began with a mission to keep the spirit of the Festival alive in Edinburgh all year round, and to stage UK productions of European avant-garde classics; at different times, it has acted as a vital outpost of experimental British Fringe theatre, as a forcing-house for new drama on its way to London, and as a venue which – during the Edinburgh Fringe – has sometimes hosted some of the most exciting and significant international work ever seen in the UK.

Yet in its essence, it has gradually become Scotland's new play theatre; the place where playwrights can be found and fostered over a period of years and decades, to the point where – using the Traverse's traditional position as a linking-point between Scottish theatre and the great international platform of the Edinburgh Festival – they can take their full place in the national and global conversation. It's thirty-five years, now, since I first started to watch theatre at the Traverse; and here, in celebration, are a few distilled memories of moments when the work made or fostered there has changed me, decisively, and for good. In some cases, I know that others have had the same experience, and undergone the same revelatory shifts in consciousness; in others, I can only guess that I was not alone, and that the ripple effects spreading from those small theatre spaces were significant. I am sure, though, that all the playwrights mentioned here should be recognised and celebrated, as brave and eloquent exponents of the art of making new imaginative worlds; including – on occasions, and often incidentally – new possible Scotlands, or new ways of being Scottish, in our time.

1978–82 John Byrne *The Slab Boys Trilogy*

This was the moment, decisive for me and many in my generation, when I first knew, not only intellectually but with heart, mind and soul, that Scotland was a place not fixed in the past, but blazing on into the future, with a voice of its own. John Byrne's great postwar trilogy – beginning with a workplace drama set in the in 'slab room' of a Paisley carpet factory in 1957, then moving on to the staff dance and to a local graveyard, fifteen years later – was in a sense a strange play to achieve this momentous shift. It represented the climax of a ten-year revolution in Scottish theatre and other arts, which began far from the Traverse, with a smash-hit 1972 Fringe event called *The Great Northern Welly Boot Show*, which brought together a crucial change-making generation of postwar Scottish artists, musicians and performers. Among those involved were Billy Connolly as performer, Kenny Ireland as performer and director, John Byrne as designer, and Tom McGrath as musical director. Within a year, John McGrath of the radical left-wing theatre company 7:84 had launched his Scottish company, built around the same core of artists, and was heading out on tour with *The Cheviot, the Stag and the Black, Black Oil*; and by the mid-1970s Chris Parr, a new Traverse director with a special commitment to Scottish work, was starting to commission plays from McGrath, Connolly and Byrne.

Byrne's first Traverse play, *The Slab Boys*, when it finally appeared in 1978, was less experimental than the thrilling, jazz-inflected, abstract work Tom McGrath was producing at the Traverse by that time, and less surreal in its comic concept that Byrne's own first play, *Writer's Cramp*; some critics even mistook its lurid proto-post-modern attention to cultural detail for dour workplace naturalism, in the tradition of – for example – Roddy MacMillan's *The Bevellers*, seen at the Lyceum in the 1970s. Byrne, though, was a dramatic poet whose fast-moving, detail-studded, highly coloured and hilariously comic stage language breathed life into a wholly new idea of Scotland, irreverent, unafraid, culturally diverse, plugged into world culture, and no longer remotely intimidated by conventional British norms. His characters are Catholic boys from Ferguslie Park, on the loose in what was once Presbyterian Scotland, their minds full of dramatic and sensual religious imagery; their cultural inspirations come from the European avant-garde, and from American rock 'n' roll.

And in looking so clearly, fearlessly and humorously at the detail of the cultural lives of his own generation, Byrne not only played a key role in setting Scotland free from the externally imposed myths and half-truths about its identity that had defined the nation for two centuries and more. He also spoke for a great and decisive shift in world culture, the moment when it began to be clear that the homogenising, centralising and standardising impulse of modernism and modernity was not enough; and that diversity, detail, and cultural specificity mattered as a source of truth and energy, and of new kinds of futures of which the metropolitan centres as yet knew little.

1982 Liz Lochhead *Blood And Ice*

Following the 1979 Scottish Referendum debacle – when the idea of devolution was approved by a majority of voters, but not by a big enough margin to satisfy Westminster – the terrific energy that had surrounded the debate on Scotland's future in the 1970s disapppeared for a while, despite the continuing economic bonanza of North Sea oil; John Byrne completed his *Slab Boys* trilogy in 1982, with the notably romantic and lyrical graveyard drama *Still Life*, but could hardly have started it in those subdued times. The postwar meritocratic generation of Scottish writers, though, were not to be stopped; and in the early 1980s, Chris Parr's Traverse successor Peter Lichtenfels made a huge effort to disrupt the traditional masculine bias in Scotland's sense of itself by fostering female writers, including Marcella Evaristi, Rona Munro and the woman who is now Scotland's national Makar, Liz Lochhead.

Lochhead was a poet by trade and a close cultural friend of many of the Seventies generation of Traverse playwrights; but in 1982, when she was in her mid-thirties, she exploded into the world of theatre with a terrific piece of feminist and post-feminist theatre called *Blood and Ice*, about the writer Mary Shelley, and her creation of the story of *Frankenstein*. *Blood and Ice* is not a notably Scottish play; Lochhead's fierce theatrical love-affair with new forms of Scots language, which was to produce texts like her brilliant version of *Tartuffe* and her 1987 masterpiece, *Mary Queen of Scots Got Her Head Chopped Off*, was still a few years away. It is, though, a brave and passionate play of ideas, with something vital to say about the strengths and the defining weaknesses of the idea of sexual equality. For Mary – the daughter of the great feminist Mary Wollstonecraft – the Shelleyan dream of sexual freedom and liberation from bourgeois marriage, comes to mean nothing but toleration of her husband's infidelities, while she buries the babies for whom he will not provide a safe and stable home; and at a moment of low energy in Scotland's cultural life, *Blood and Ice* came as a blazing piece of work at the cutting-edge of feminist debate, made in Scotland, written for the world.

1985 Jo Clifford *Losing Venice*

By the mid-1980s, Scotland was rediscovering its political voice through the gathering rebellion against Thatcherism and all it stood for; and there was also a new mood of high confidence at the Traverse, where the young artistic director Jenny Killick, and her associate Steve Unwin, scored a huge success in 1985 when they premiered work by three brand-new Scottish-based playwrights, Peter Arnott, Chris Hannan, and Jo Clifford, then known as John Clifford. What distinguished these playwrights was the epic ambition of their work. If drama written by and about the powerless often expresses itself through workplace or domestic naturalism – the notorious 'sofa plays' and 'kitchen sink' of British domestic drama – then this new wave of Traverse writers wanted nothing to do with it; their subjects were the rise and fall of empires and the birth and death of political movements, and their style was as bold and free-flowing as Shakespeare's in the prelude to *Henry V*.

Jo Clifford's *Losing Venice*, premiered at the Traverse on 1 August 1985, is a beautiful, lyrical and epic drama about an empire – in this case the Spanish one of the late 16th century – no longer able to hold on to its far-flung foreign possessions, and about the impact of that politics of decline on a cast of ordinary and less-ordinary characters. Its success was huge and immediate, and the play went on to travel the world; early in 1986, I remember watching the Traverse production played under unfamiliar stars, at the Perth Festival in Western Australia. Along with Arnott's *White Rose* – about a Russian woman pilot of the Soviet era – and Hannan's *Elizabeth Gordon Quinn*, a political drama in expressionist style set during the Glasgow Rent Strike of 1914, *Losing Venice* was part of one of the most exciting and game-changing of all Traverse festival seasons; and the fact that the play has never been revived since, on any Scottish main stage, remains one of the enduring mysteries of Scottish theatrical life.

1995 David Greig – Suspect Culture / *One Way Street*

Across the UK, the drama of the 1990s was said to be about 'in yer face' theatre; a kind of drama, most famously represented by Mark Ravenhill's *Shopping and Fucking*, that sought to strip away the surface of British life during a long economic boom, and to reveal the underlying violence of the culture. The Traverse played a significant role in developing 'in yer face' theatre, not least through its relationship with Anthony Neilson, the London-based son of Scottish actors Sandy Neilson and Beth Robens, who became one of the pioneers of a theatre quite relentless in its exploration of violence. And Ian

Brown, director of the Traverse from 1988 to 1996, directed the original stage version of Irvine Welsh's mid-1990s masterpiece, *Trainspotting*, with its gleeful celebration of a generation determined to make its mark on the world not by conforming to the bourgeois norms of consumer society, but by leaving behind a foetid trail of body fluids, on the way to glorious self-destruction.

Although they were often swept into the 'in-yer-face' bracket, though, the Traverse writers who emerged during the 1990s – David Greig, David Harrower, Nicola McCartney, and later Henry Adam and many others – were generally of a more meditative and even elegiac turn of mind. Harrower's *Knives in Hens*, premiered at the Traverse in 1995, is a strange, timeless tale about the shift from tradition to modernity, which rapidly became an international contemporary classic; and David Greig's early plays – *Stalinland* and *Europe*, among others – were bold, big-minded, heartfelt attempts to come to grips with the political changes sweeping the continent, after 1989.

It was at the quiet Traverse press night of *One Way Street*, though, that I first fully felt what Greig and Suspect Culture – the company he had co-founded with director Graham Eatough – were doing with the stuff of late 20th century theatre. *One Way Street* is a simple monologue of lost love, intercut with a deep sense of 20th century politics and place, and set on the streets of Berlin; but in a merging of media that was to become characteristic of their work, Suspect Culture illustrated it with a series of still images of the back streets of Edinburgh, instantly recognisable, yet suddenly given resonance, and a whole new dimension of melancholy universality, as they stepped into the role of fractured Berlin. The hallmark of Suspect Culture – which finally dissolved itself in 2009, after twenty years of huge achievement – was always this brooding, late 20th century internationalism, this preoccupation with the life of a planet increasing interconnected through air travel and electronic communications, yet increasingly fragmented in terms of people's ability to make real emotional connections. The subject matter was not particularly Scottish, but the voice often was, a supremely confident and beautiful global voice, created here.

As for Greig himself, his work with Suspect Culture – lyrical, beautiful, and collaborative – was always only one strand of a breathtakingly productive career, which has ranged from solid, ambitious one-off Traverse dramas – *The Architect*, *The Speculator*, *Outlying Islands* – to sharp cabaret pieces written for election-day performances at the Traverse, and one exquisite, light-touch political fantasy about Edinburgh, *Caledonia Dreaming*, presented on the eve of the devolution referendum of 1997. He has collaborated with rock musicians and choreographers, on works like the delicious Edinburgh mini-musical *Midsummer*, now an international hit, and *San Diego*, a great, ambitious global epic, staged at the Edinburgh Festival of 2003. He has written superb plays for young people, from *Dr Korczak's Example* in 2001 to *The Monster in the Hall* in 2010. Through the British Council, he has worked with young playwrights across the Arab world, foreshadowed the Arab Spring in his own writing, curated a season about it in Scotland; he is the writer behind two hugely successful current National Theatre of Scotland shows, the Borders-ballad-based pub play *The Strange Undoing of Prudencia Hart*, and the Citizens' Theatre co-production *Glasgow Girls*, Cora Bissett's popular musical about the struggle against Britain's inhumane asylum laws. His biography reads, in other words, like a one-man history of Scottish theatre since 1990, of its growing range, diversity and confidence, of the key role of the Traverse in that development, and of the impact of the coming of the National Theatre of Scotland, in 2006; and Greig, at forty-four, is still only at the start of his creative career.

2006 Gregory Burke *Black Watch*

The date was 6 August 2006, the place was the Drill Hall in Forrest Road Edinburgh; and the production – created by the brand new National Theatre of Scotland, directed by John Tiffany, and presented as part of that year's Traverse Fringe programme – was *Black Watch*, the mighty and spectacular verbatim drama, based on the playwright Gregory Burke's interviews with Scottish soldiers who had served in Iraq, that has gone on to make the global reputation of the brand new National Theatre of Scotland, and has – to date – been seen across four continents, and has played to almost a quarter of a million theatre people, winning premier theatre awards in Sydney and New York.

If *Black Watch* is an NTS production, though, Gregory Burke is very much a Traverse playwright, and *Black Watch* the living expression of the way in which the Traverse – its body of plays and playwrights, build up over forty years – became one of the foundation-stones of the NTS. At the turn of the millennium, the script for Burke's first produced play, *Gagarin Way* – a thrilling variation, set in a computer factory in Fife, on the end of meaningful left-wing politics in Britain, and of the morbid symtpoms of that decline – was plucked from the unsolicited script pile at the Traverse by John Tiffany (then associate to Philip Howard, Traverse artistic director from 1996 until 2007); in 2001, it put Burke – then working as a dishwasher and hotel porter – at the centre of one of the most thrilling Traverse first nights of the last twenty years.

Gregory Burke is not the most experimental of recent Traverse writers. But he speaks for working-class Scotland in a voice that is instantly recognised on its streets and in its bars. And in John Tiffany, he found a director who could work – with musicians, designers, with the choreographer Steven Hoggett – to bring out not only the humour, the toughness, the incipient violence of that voice, but its hidden emotion and lyricism, in a world-class piece of theatre that soars in one hundred minutes from the intensely specific to the absolutely universal, and is still touring the world, almost seven years on.

2012 Morna Pearson *The Artist Man and the Mother Woman*

So the Traverse moves on into the 21st century; and one of the most exciting new voices to emerge there in the last half-decade belongs to Morna Pearson, a young playwright from Elgin who writes in a kind of day-glo Doric, a lurid 21st century version of the strong Scots language of the Mearns and the north east. Her first short play, *Distracted*, was seen at the Traverse in 2006 as part of a joint season of short new plays co-produced with the NTS; and at the end of 2012, her full-length piece *The Artist Man and the Mother Woman* – a kind of theatrical slasher-movie set in a small north-east coastal town – was the first full Traverse production by the theatre's new artistic director, Orla O'Loughlin, only the second woman to hold the job.

Pearson's work is saturated in the sensibility of a generation obsessed with the resurgence of both grotesque social inequality, and extreme sexual neuroses, in a society that once thought it had begun to solve both problems; this is theatre from the age of *Little Britain*, but expressed in a language that sets up huge, productive tensions with the couthy imagery traditionally associated with rural Scotland. On the big stage of Traverse One, it emerged as a superbly strange and vivid piece of drama, illuminated – like so many previous Traverse shows – by five bold actors without whom none of the above would be possible; in this case Anne Lacey, Garry Collins, Molly

Innes, Lewis Howden and Lynn Kennedy. And meanwhile, in Traverse Two, a new touring company from the Borders was presenting Blythe Duff in a brilliant revival of *Iron*, Rona Munro's 2002 Traverse two-hander about crime, motherhood and punishment, now reborn a decade on, and thrilling audiences across Scotland – or subtly changing the way they see themselves and the world, and their capacity to speak of it, in their own voice.

Being Back:
Some Haggises We Would Like to Hunt Again

Ordinarily, *Edinburgh Review* would have a section where writers (poets and novelists in the main) review each other's work. Which of course works fine for our theatre issue. Except, of course, playwrights rarely formally review each other's work in print. Rather than ponder why this should be the case, we asked a number of practitioners to argue for a revival of a piece of new writing in Scotland they had – or wish they had – seen. This idea is inspired by both the Encore Revivals section of the online *Encore Theatre Magazine* website (which includes arguments for Chris Hannan's *The Evil Doers*), and 'The Visitors' rehearsed readings, for which a theatre professional would choose a play to direct and introduce. Like those enterprises, this section is the start of the conversation and the list in no way definitive or even defined...

Nicola McCartney & K.S. Morgan McKean

Dark Earth by David Harrower
First performed at the Traverse Theatre, Edinburgh, July/August 2003

My reasons for wishing to see *Dark Earth* revived are personal. Of all the great – or almost great? – Scottish plays from the last, say, twenty years, this in my view is 'the one that got away'. And unfortunately for me, this was in large part because I directed the premiere production of it and made too many errors for the play to survive unscathed. I don't mean to suggest it was all my fault; it wasn't. But few new plays are director-proof and I simply got this one wrong. Because I'm convinced that there is a great play somewhere inside *Dark Earth*, I bristle with annoyance at my part in its relative lack of success. I'd love a chance to put it right.

Dark Earth takes the form, classically, of a comedy. A young couple from Glasgow go on a drive one weekend out to the Roman remains of the Antonine Wall in West Lothian. Their car breaks down and they are stranded, without even a mobile phone, and are thrown on to the mercy of a local farming family with whom they end up spending the night. The family of mother, father and daughter have their own tensions, their economic situation is increasingly fraught, and over the course of a mere twenty-four hours, relations between the urban day-trippers and rural family deteriorate to a point where the former are practically run off the farm.

On the playwright's part it was an ingenuous attempt to take a searching look at the extraordinary challenges of a contemporary rural farming life in the Scotland of the time. That topicality has not diminished in the decade since. But if I'm making it sound like an issue play, it isn't. Among the play's many counter-virtues are the significance of the setting: the borders of West Lothian and Lanarkshire are one of the few places in Lowland Scotland that are neither East nor West. As the daughter, Christine, remarks: 'slap bang in the middle'. And there is a running theme of history living through us: Petey, the father, is a self-taught authority on the Roman colonisation of Scotland and also on Charles Edward Stuart, the Young Pretender. There is a fascinating and truly theatrical idea deep in the heart of the play that the farming family should embody all their own history of place. I always privately believed that they were ghosts and we staged the moment at the end of the play, where the family pelt the couple's repaired/departing car with stones, as if they were the Votadini tribe repelling the invading Romans. But it was too little, too late – and one of the lessons I learned is that if, as a director, you're keeping a secret from the audience, then it ain't going to work…

While I'm in the confessional, I'll add that the production's major error was to make the urban couple more affluent and middle-class than Harrower had intended them to be. Of course being a British play, you can't escape having to make a choice about 'class', but you still have to make the right one. I hasten to add that none of this was the fault of the two fine actors, but by making them a bit posher than they were meant to be, it turned partly into a comedy of manners between them and the farmers, which inevitably distracted all of us – acting company, playwright and audience – from the essential and purer concept of an urban and rural divide at the heart of the play.

Finally, and I think Harrower would allow this, we both got too bogged down in detail and the result was too tame. For example, there is clearly an attraction between Euan from the city and Christine the daughter. In Act Three Christine decides she is going to run away from the claustrophobia of her family and Euan initially aids her. But we were so keen to get the *argument* of the play correct that we forgot about the sex.

So that's why my reasons are personal. It is very aggravating to have got a play wrong when you're (still) convinced that there's a great play in there. I would love love love to get the chance to see it done again. Better. Preferably by me.

Philip Howard

Come And Be Killed by Stanley Eveling
First performed at the Traverse Theatre, 1967

BETTINA **[gloomily]** *There's not much love around here, is there?*[1]

Bettina, I've got a lot of love for you, and there's plenty others I bet would too – it's just that nobody's seen you around these parts since 1967, leastways not outside the pages of a script. Which is really just far too damn bad for all concerned.

Superficially, the plot of *Come And Be Killed* is fairly straightforward – Jim, whose job is editing the first third of an encyclopaedia (*'From A to I I'm a very enlightened person. It all goes a bit dark after that'*,[2] a mordant touch that pretty well sums him up) cajoles the virginal and wisely sceptical Bettina into sex, after which she falls pregnant. Jim then embarks upon a series of escalating manouevres intended to sway Bettina towards an abortion (including coolly plotting a seduction of his best friend Jerry's wife Christine precisely when he knows Bettina will come home and catch them). This ever-intensifying anti-charm offensive culminates in his throwing a booze-sluiced party intended to celebrate Bettina's return from the termination (to which he naturally does not accompany her). It's not my place to spoil the conclusion, but suffice to say that disturbing imagery ensues.

There are any number of plays which confidently proffer as part of their thesis the not-massively-contentious observation that men can really be slime, but few in such enthrallingly subversive fashion as this one. For starters, it's an overtly comedic piece of writing, brutal subject matter notwithstanding. For another thing, despite the laughs continuously engendered throughout, it's also undeniably as sad as hell.

It's furthermore refreshing in allowing each of its four characters a cogent, coherent viewpoint, both upon the world of the play at large and the particular dilemma that lies at its heart, that of abortion. Each of these individual perspectives clashes with those of the others, often dissonantly, but the way Mr Eveling renders them, none is there merely as a makeweight or to play the clear antagonist to a 'correct' point of view. For example, while Jim's behaviour throughout the course of the play can often be outright repugnant, his rationalisations for his actions are typically well-considered and confidently articulated, to the extent of being, arguably, sporadically seductive.

Why, though, exhume this play in particular, and why now? First off, because it's a stronger, more nuanced, more affecting piece of work than most any other Scottish play I'm aware of. It does plenty to recommend itself through its possession of real muscular intensity of language, finding expression via striking thoughts and imagery uttered in linguistically inventive and memorable ways. The odd fleeting mockery of advertising lingo notwithstanding, the characters in *Come And Be Killed* are so far from speaking in banal televisual-style clichés that they come across like people who never even watch TV in the first place.

Most of all, though, a revival would serve as a choice and wonderful example to a younger generation of playwrights (and audiences, directors, actors) of how to write a play about a social issue of import without falling into the trap of ending up having written an 'issue play' – i.e. one where genuinely narratively dramatic elements ultimately end up grossly subordinate to the weight and primacy accorded the simple existence of the core issue itself, as opposed to the rare and welcome work such as Mr Eveling's here where the inverse occurs. Its focus is far more this one particular situation involving these four especial people than being any form of morally prescriptive tract upon the issue of abortion as a whole, and it's precisely this specificity which is the play's great strength. It doesn't send an audience out incanting the same well-crafted uniform message-speech they've all just been simultaneously served up. Rather it presents a carefully calibrated aesthetic experience which, while theatrically direct and communicative, is also not afraid to be healthily ambiguous and complex, that flips any number of different switches in any number of different people, requiring each to process what they've just witnessed in their own idiosyncratic way.

If you were to say to me that this is what theatre should do, I'd agree with you. If you were to then suggest that this is what most current homegrown theatre actually does do – well, no, not so much.

This is a play which I contend could – and should – be given the opportunity to inspire, amuse, appal, confuse and sicken a whole new lucky generation (myself included, said play being a good dozen years older than I am). It's crying out to be dragged back onstage to live. As Jim proclaims, *"'I love you' is never an expression of feeling. It's a declaration of intent.'*[3]

Come And Be Killed, I love you.

Alan McKendrick

Notes

The quotes used are all from *Eveling, Come And Be Killed & Dear Janet Rosenberg, Dear Mr Kooning*, Calder & Boyars, London, 1971): 1– p. 36; 2 – p. 20; 3 – p.19.

Shining Souls by Chris Hannan
First produced at the Traverse, 1996. Revived at the Tron Theatre, 2003

When I first saw *Shining Souls* at the Tron in 2003 I was blown away by its humanity, and its gentle spiritual heart. The title fits perfectly – the characters shine out in a luminous fashion and I can't think of another Scottish play like it for its sheer array of wonderfully complex, fucked-up and deliciously compelling beings. But they aren't just shining people – they are the shining *souls* of the title, and it's here that I think the play most shows its genius. In every encounter and every situation there is an understated but pervading spirituality that entices and draws the audience in. Some of the characters yearn for something beyond, others are running away from it. Catholicism, tarot cards, even the finding of a never-heard-of Tom Jones CD may or may not offer what is being looked for, but by the end of the play they, and we, have come via a carnival-like ending to some sort of transformation.

The piece has aspects of a Greek play; there is deep tragedy in the background – a double suicide of two young men and a heroine who can't escape from it, and it requires intervention to move her and the whole situation forward. The language is realistic but also has a poetry to it that means we are in a heightened and theatrical place, hilarious at times, dark at others. It's a really hard trick to pull off in a modern play, particularly a modern play set in the gritty back streets of the Glasgow Barras, but Chris Hannan does it effortlessly.

All in all *Shining Souls* has a certain lunacy to it, a feeling that in this place and with these people anything could happen. And it does. The production I saw had Kath Howden in the lead, and when I re-read it now I can't not think of her. It seems that the casting was perfect – Ann has the mix of bonkers impulsiveness combined with regret and being slightly lost that Kath brings in spades.

The First Act opens with Ann and her daughter Mandy who is trying to read her tarot cards in hope that they might illuminate which choice Ann should make. It turns out this is Ann's wedding day, and she is engaged to someone called Billy – all fine, except there's another man on the scene, also called Billy, and it was this Billy that Ann has spent the night with. Not only that, she's asked the second Billy to move in with her, and he's going to arrive any moment with his suitcases, probably at much the same time as the first Billy and the priest turn up for the marriage ceremony. We come to learn that Ann lost both of her sons from suicide, and we understand that the two

Billies in some way replace them, albeit in a way that creates emotional chaos for those around her.

The next character we meet is Charlie, a waster and small-time con-man and his side-kick, Max. Charlie turns up at his ex-wife's door needing some money – he has slept rough and is looking for a tenner. When she's reluctant to give it to him, he invents the tale of his mother's imminent demise, saying he needs the money to get to the hospital in time – a story that has both him and the ex-wife Margaret Mary in tears. As he leaves with the tenner in his pocket, he hears from his brother that his mother is in fact really dying, suddenly and unexpectedly, but rather than going to see her, Charlie spends the day looking for the perfect suit. And then there is Prophet John and Nanette, who we first meet in the marketplace of the Barras. Nanette is trying to sell CDs to anyone and everyone, Prophet John is hunted by the spirit and wishes he didn't have to be the one to gives prophesies – prophesies that, we discover, tell us more about John himself than anyone else.

Without giving the plot away, these ten original and wonderful characters get caught up in each other's almost farce-like vortex and chaos ensues on this balmy, hot day in the Barras. All day the wardrobe in which Ann's sons hanged themselves watches over everything; at times it's a shrine, at times an unmentionable but all-pervading presence, at times simply a place to hide. It is also beautifully balanced – because this is a play full of symmetry – by the new wardrobe bought in the Barras and moved around good-naturedly by the rivalling Billies.

In the Second Act the spiritual yearning of the characters comes to the fore, and the other side seems nearer still. Ann gets the answer she was looking for and a release from the past. The jamboree and the rituals of the day take us somewhere, and as the play closes, you feel a new beginning. A slightly odd and alternative new beginning, but certainly a new beginning.

Zinnie Harris

Good by C.P. Taylor
First produced by the Royal Shakespeare Company, 1981; revived at the Tron Theatre, 1992

Sometimes when I'm doing my tax return, I look at theatre tickets for shows I've seen in the last eighteen months or so and have no memory of them. But I can still remember *Good*, which I saw twenty-one years ago at The Tron Theatre. Not the actors, which is unusual for me, but the story. So it must have been the play itself which made an impact.

Basically we see our protagonist, who at the beginning of the play seems a perfectly normal family man, a music lover, and then, over the course of the evening, before our eyes he becomes a Nazi. And we can understand how it happened. I can't remember how Taylor does it, but he does. It's a story for all times. When I read the script of *The Last King of Scotland*, which was about a doctor who worked for and then became entangled with Idi Amin and his regime, I remarked to the director that it reminded me of *Good*. I didn't expect him to have seen the play but he had, and we discussed it enthusiastically. He too saw great similarities between *Good* and the film that he was about to make.

On the first Christmas Eve of the 1914–18 war, it's said that soldiers from both sides met on no-man's land. They smoked together, played football and sang hymns. Next day they were ordered to go back and kill each other. Apparently, they were never again allowed to fraternise at Christmas – the top brass feared their men would refuse to fight if they got to know the 'enemy'. I can't hear that story but an indescribable feeling grips me – maybe Munch's *Scream* comes close to capturing what I feel. That is the awful territory that Taylor is exploring… how did we come to this? How could this happen? Does it begin with a small, seemingly insignificant, event?

It's been said before but… if we don't understand why people do evil we have no hope of preventing it in the future. Next year is the one hundredth anniversary of the outbreak of the 1914–18 war (I don't see how it can be called a world war when quite a few countries were not involved). The number of deaths from that conflict is estimated at thirty-seven million. And people want to celebrate this?

I'd love to see C.P. Taylor's *Good* again, because I think he shows us how we have to be responsible for all our actions, that everything we do, or don't do, has a consequence. And that is something that I would like to be reminded of.

This is making *Good* sound solemn, but it wasn't. There was lots of music (a brass band) and it was very entertaining. Of course, you wouldn't expect anything else with Michael Boyd directing.

Well, I have just looked it up on-line… I am reminded how hilarious John Sampson was, dressed in Bavarian leather shorts and doing one of those thigh-slapping routines; and yes, someone (Jimmy Chisholm?) did a Marlene Dietrich impersonation, and Ronny Letham (R.I.P.) and Edith Macarthur were in the cast too. The set was pretty amazing, with lots of doors which were used cleverly.

Good seems to have stuck in my mind because of the emotions it aroused. But whatever it was it's just one of the shows I will always remember.

Anne Lacey

The Great Northern Welly Boot Show by Billy Connolly and Tom Buchan
First produced at Waverley Market, 1972

The summer of 1972. Waverley Market, now Princes Mall, Edinburgh. For the admission price of 75p, you enter the cavernous space to a rock band playing. A show begins at 7.30 but mainly at 8 – the posters had the time wrong. That poster shows a long-haired, bearded young man wearing a pierrot clown costume (no hat) making the two-fingered peace sign, with a voluptuous blonde in hotpants and thigh-high platform boots running away from him. The hairy boy's boots have wings.

The Great Northern Welly Boot Show, by Billy Connolly and Tom Buchan. Directed by Robin Lefevre. Nightly 8pm, matinees 2.30 Wed & Sat. 21 Aug to 8 Sept.

And that's it – that is all the physical evidence of this play I can find, other than four photographs of the performance. No published script, no YouTube clip. And this a show that launched a comedy god, gave the world a song celebrating wellies, showcased a myriad of brilliant actors and musicians, and led to a pair of boots shaped like bananas to be so culturally iconic that they now reside in a museum. Above all, it inspired a generation of theatre makers to the possibilities. And it was a hit.

Words like 'groundbreaking', 'a linchpin', 'vital', 'the power of popular theatre', 'addressing contemporary socio-political issues,' 'outrageous', crop up when looking/googling for this play. But no play itself.

I have performed in and seen a lot of comic plays that truly deserve another airing. But I began to think what really is the ultimate show I would have liked to have seen and would actually love to see again and just what the hell was it about? 'Welly Boot' feels like mystery, but a big, successful, funny one. And like a welly-wearing fairy godfather to what came after.

Here is the scant knowledge I can gain. The play was a satire, loosely based on the upper Clydeside 'work in' led by Jimmy Reid, reset to a Wellington boot factory. It was first performed at the King's Theatre, Glasgow, as part of the Clyde Fair Festival (a precursor to Mayfest) on 26 June 1972, directed then by Tony Palmer. It was such a success it was felt by all involved it needed to go on again, redirected by Robin Lefevre. A co-operative of friends, a lot from the then Citizens' Theatre for Youth, called themselves the Offshore Theatre Company. Every mep183mber would have a share in the box office.

Two months after the King's performance, the show played the Edinburgh Fringe Festival.

John Bett told me – 'We actually all did make money from it.'

He had memories of – 'Interminable meetings, meetings meetings. We were trying to be socialists in a collective.' Indeed at one of these meetings, it was agreed that the Offshore Theatre Company would stage a protest by doing a sit-in at that bastion of capitalist imperialism, STV.

Marilyn Imrie remortgaged the flat she shared with Kenny Ireland to fund the performances. As did Tom Buchan. Many others also chipped in money.

But what of the play? These are the snatches I've gathered:

– As well as topical politics, it is a love story between leading man Billy Connolly and Leslie Mackie characters.

– Hamish Imlach's character is given a golden welly as his pay-off for fifty years of service.

– Juliet Cadzow sings to the tune of *Love Letters*, 'When wellies are next to my skin, that's when the good times begin, who needs champagne vintage wine, when you can make love to a big size nine.'

– Two giant heads of Harold Wilson and Ted Heath, created by John Byrne, dance a striptease with a professional stripper called Brandy Di Frank.

– Police were called.

John Bett – 'It was a mess of agitprop politics and daft songs – popular enjoyable theatre that was one step above cabaret. But it was zeitgeisty. And a formative experience for everyone in a new kind of theatre.'

Marilyn Imrie – 'We all, in a way, I think became bonded for life. It was a political play and a good night out. John Byrne's giant heads danced with the stripper symbolising politicians seduced by sex, money and power - who used Scotland as a puppet.'

After the initial police intervention at a striptease onstage, two policemen arrived every night at the same time – 'We're here to check everything's OK' – precisely when Brandy performed. Marilyn Imrie who, as front of house, had to let them in, says ironically – 'We did a great service in keeping the local constabulary happy.'

The play immediately transferred to the Young Vic in London. It was a huge success. (Brandy Di Frank was unable to do the London run and was replaced with a fellow stripper – a transsexual called Keith.) The official Edinburgh Festival promptly commissioned a show from the Offshore Theatre Company for the following year.

However, sitting in the audience at Edinburgh run was John McGrath and the MacLennans. McGrath promptly nabbed the actors Bett, Alex Norton and Bill Patterson, the musician Alan Ross and MacLennan went on to marry

Cadzow and her welly-loving ways.

Welly Boot was a celebration of direct action – through scenes, songs and sketches, and audience address. John McGrath had found the people he was looking for. The following year they produced *The Cheviot the Stag and the Black Black Oil*.

Tom McGrath, the musical director of the show, had found possibility – theatre would now become his main focus, after adventures with the *International Times*, R.D. Laing and Trocchi. He would soon open The Third Eye Centre and be theatrical midwife to generation after generation's ideas and hopes. Oh, and write plays as well.

John Byrne's giant heads of Heath and Wilson were ceremoniously set ablaze, on a beach near Edinburgh on Hogmanay, two years later.

The co-author, the poet and playwright Tom Buchan, continued a firebrand existence, writing and living in Findhorn.

The other co-author, the shipyard worker Billy Connolly, so inspired by lifelong friend Jimmy Reid to write the play, went on to two write two further plays – for the Royal Court and for the Traverse.

But remember, John Byrne's poster had the performance time wrong. So Billy Connolly filled in the extra half hour needed by going out and doing his small folk act while the audience took their seats. And he unleashed on 400 unsuspecting fringe theatre-goers his retelling of the Crucifixion – 'and in He comes, with the long dress, and the casual sandals, and the aura… aw roon.' He was to fly, as his winged boots depict on the poster.

But it seems everyone involved in *The Great Northern Welly Boot Show* flew. I was born in 1972. I wish I'd seen it. I wish I could read it. But maybe, like all great comedy, it's mercury, and you can't catch it.

Gabriel Quigley
With thanks to Marilyn Imrie, John Bett and David Harrower.

Distracted by Morna Pearson
First produced at the Traverse Theatre, 2006

My friend the playwright, actor and contrarian David Ireland (who was in the original production of *Distracted*) once said of Morna Pearson that she is like the Dr Dre of Scottish theatre: 'She only drops an album every ten years but when she does it's a game changer.'

Her debut play *Distracted, The Chronic* for our metaphorical purposes, gave notice of an extraordinary talent. Nominated for Best Play at the Critics Awards for Theatre in Scotland 2006; the original production (as part of the Traverse 2006 Tilt season) was directed by Lorne Campbell and the cast was David Ireland, Gary Collins, Abigail Davies and Anne Lacey. The play won Morna the prestigious Meyer Whitworth Award in 2007 and has since become a touchstone for young Scots-bred playwrights. Yet it has been seen by barely a thousand people.

The play tells the story of oddball Jamie Purdy and his gran, new arrivals in a run-down caravan park in the north east of Scotland, and their boisterous neighbors George Michael (not the singer) and his mum, Bunny – a potty-mouthed, Elgin-built Blanche Dubois. Morna's writing is at once hauntingly poetic and scabrously funny. She cuts to the heart of the human condition and has a singular world view that is both bleak and optimistic.

Oh god… I want to start over. This is making me want to pull my own skin off – 'both bleak and optimistic'… yeuch. Seriously? 'both bleak and optimistic'?

That is not to diminish my endless adoration of *Distracted*, however. I really would love to see the play remounted because I've only seen it read, never in full production. I just don't really know what the best way to make a case for *Distracted* is. When I was encouraging my girlfriend to read it I just said 'You should read *Distracted*, it's really smutty.' I know how to pitch to her interests. I'm not sure I'm quite as in tune with what will attract the readership of *Edinburgh Review* and so – you should just read the play. It's published in Nick Hern's *New Scottish Plays* which includes several of my favourite plays. And I'm not even published by Nick Hern so have no dog in this fight. Or play in that book.

Maybe I should also mention that *Distracted* is important and deserving of a remount because it is written in a Doric voice we hear too little of on stage. And that it's a notable play because Morna is a young woman and young women are shamefully under-represented amongst all the middle-aged Davids that dominate Scottish theatre. Those arguments make it sound worthy, though, and *Distracted* is not a worthy play. It's the kind of play you could take a friend to who doesn't like the theatre. It's like a McJT LeRoy novel with a twist of *Viz*. Morna's plays are hilarious and tragic like The Pixies' songs are quiet then loud. And there's something peculiarly exhilarating about the two jutting against each other, it's such a satisfying tension.

Distracted is an achingly funny, heartbreakingly sad play. It is moving and true and really does have much to say to us about the human condition. It is written by a young writer of fierce talent, singular vision and voluminous wit. Scottish audiences deserve to see it remounted. So much of what we are presented with is achingly ordinary and *Distracted* is not – *Distracted* is special. I do not think we are a country so rich in theatrical gems that we can afford to leave one in our national drawer.

D.C. Jackson

The Widows of Clyth By Donald Campbell
First performed at the Traverse, 1979

Looking back over the many and varied riches of Scottish Theatre of the last twenty to thirty years, I was amazed to see how many plays are hidden away and all but forgotten, how many have never even had a professional production for years. Some are 'of their time' and may feel dated for an audience today, but there are also many that deserve to be revived. *The Widows of Clyth* by Donald Campbell is definitely one I'd love to see again, it blew a fresh wind through the Scottish Theatre of the late 1970s / early 1980s with defiantly strong female characters in the lead roles telling a story in a rural voice from the coast of Caithness in north east Scotland, a far, far cry from the predominance of the male urban plays from Scotland's Central Belt.

My copy, from a production I had directed with drama students at Queen Margaret University over twenty years ago, is buried somewhere among my books and scripts, deep in storage pending an imminent move, and I wanted to find another one so I could read it again. I tried various bookshops with no luck, I looked for a copy on that vast enterprise named after a South American river – to no avail. I asked friends, tried libraries, the universities – nothing. Eventually, after weeks of searching online, I tracked a copy down. A disgraceful comment, I think, on the low regard we have for our playwrighting and our theatrical heritage.

Donald Campbell was born in Caithness and clearly grew up with the stories and accounts surrounding the disaster etched into his heart. *The Widows of Clyth* is a play of two Acts written in 1979 based on the real-life events surrounding the Wick fishing disaster of 1876, when *The Inflexible* sank on the rocks in a fierce storm with no survivors; four of those men lost were brothers and between the six men drowned that day they left five widows and twenty-six children destined for acute hardship without the mainstay of their income from fishing.

From the first off-stage scream we know this isn't going to be a night of comedy, and in fact the tragedy cranks up at the sight of Betsy and Keet Sutherland half dragging, half holding up their sister-in-law Helen, shuddering under the shock of the news her husband is drowned from the wreck of the boat he fishes with his brothers. The tension builds and builds throughout the first scene as we learn one woman after the other has lost her husband, her child's father, and young Keet has lost even the promise of that with the death of her betrothed. Bonded in their loss but alone in their grief, the terrible reality slowly dawns on the women, they now face poverty because the land they've crofted for generations is too meagre to support them and they will be forced to leave to go to live in an unfamiliar town and run a boarding-house or sweetie-shop.

This, though, is a play about the survival and determination of the women. Against the norms of the day, all advice and protestations they would starve the widows worked the barren land, eking out their income with seasonal gutting and any labour they could get, so they could keep their homes and land for their children just as it had been passed onto them.

The Widows Of Clyth is a powerful drama made all the more so because it is truth not fiction, but what immediately grabbed me is there are five strong female roles and therefore five good parts for women in a drama told by them and about them, unusual for Scottish plays at that time when male characters and male stories dominated.

The play revolves around the characters led by Betsy Sutherland, a heroic figure of great dignity – widow to skipper Donald Sutherland, her young sister, Keet, Helen, Annie and Chrissie, widows to the other Sutherland brothers, their personal issues of living with death and the very real consequences of the Clyth fishing disaster. Entering in and out of their croft and their lives are Hector, the youngest Sutherland brother who survived the storm aboard his boat, *The Dauntless*; George Clyne, consumed with guilt because he slept in that morning, missing the boat, and now feels forever beholden to the widows; and Markie, a carter from Wick who brings light relief along with the daily newspaper.

Having read *The Widows Of Clyth* again after twenty years, I was surprised by the strength of it and how contemporary the relationships between the women are. The dialogue is at first reading deceptively domestic, swinging between conflict and humour, but the unspoken subtext masks the severity of the womens' deep grief.

Donald Campbell should be rightly proud of this play, but I would be interested to know if, for a modern audience, he would allow the women to speak entirely for themselves.

Alison Peebles

Notes on Contributors

Davey Anderson studied at the University of Glasgow. He is a writer, director and composer for theatre. His plays include *Snuff* and *Blackout*. His work as associate director with the National Theatre of Scotland includes *Black Watch* and *Enquirer*.

Peter Arnott began his career at the Traverse in 1985 with *The Death of Elias Sawney* and *White Rose*. The same year *The Boxer Benny Lynch* opened in Glasgow Arts Centre. Author of many plays and adaptations, in 2012 he wrote *The Infamous Brothers Davenport,* adapted Robin Jenkins' *The Conegatherers* and won a Fringe First with *Why Do You Stand There in the Rain?*

Ian Brown is playwright, poet and Kingston University's Professor in Drama. The first Chair of the SSP (1973–75), he has held that post three times since: 1984–87; 1997–99; and 2010–13. He has published widely on theatre and cultural matters and had some twenty plays produced in the UK and abroad.

Jo Clifford is a playwright and performer. She is the author of about eighty plays in every dramatic medium, including *Losing Venice* and *Tree of Knowledge*. Her *Great Expectations* is currently running in London's West End. For further details see www.teatrodomundo.com.

Zinnie Harris's multi-award winning *Further than the Furthest Thing* has been performed all over the world. Other highlights are a trilogy of plays for the RSC (*Solstice, Midwinter* and *Fall,* the latter co-produced by the Traverse Theatre), *Nightingale and Chase* for the Royal Court and a new version of Ibsen's *A Doll's House* for the Donmar Warehouse.

David Greig is a playwright and theatre maker.

Philip Howard trained as a theatre director at the Royal Court Theatre before joining the Traverse Theatre, first as Associate Director, and then from 1996–2007 as Artistic Director. He teaches MLitt in Playwriting & Dramaturgy at the University of Glasgow and is currently Chief Executive of Dundee Rep Theatre.

D.C. Jackson's plays include *My Romantic History*, *The Wall*, *The Ducky* and *The Chooky Brae*, and an adaptation of *The Marriage of Figaro*. He has been Pearson Playwright in Residence at the Royal Court Theatre, London, and has taken part in the Old Vic's 24 hour Plays Celebrity Gala.

Anne Lacey has worked for most theatre companies in Scotland including Alba, Raindog, LookOut, Communicado, Tron, Traverse, Citizens, Dundee Rep, National Theatre of Scotland, and also for the RSC, Old Vic and the National, and also in films, radio and TV, including *Harry Potter and the Goblet of Fire* and *Hamish Macbeth*.

Roddy Lumsden's most recent collections are *Terrific Melancholy* (Bloodaxe) and *The Bells of Hope* (Penned in the Margins). He is Poetry Editor for Salt and Series Editor of the Best British Poetry. He lives in London.

Nicola McCartney, a playwright, director and dramaturg from Belfast, has lived and worked in Scotland since 1990. Lecturer in Writing for Theatre and Performance at Edinburgh University, her work includes: *Heritage* (Traverse Theatre/ Faber, 2001), *Standing Wave: Delia Derbyshire in the '60s* (Tron Theatre/ Reeling & Writhing) and *A Sheep Called Skye* (National Theatre of Scotland).

Peter Mackay is a writer, academic and broadcast journalist. He is the author of *From another island* (Clutag Press, 2010) and *Sorley Maclean* (RIISS, 2010).

K.S. Morgan McKean is one of the Traverse Fifty. She is the recipient of a Playwrights' Studio Award to develop her new play, *Somewhere Else*. Her work includes: *Becoming* (lookOUT) and *Beneath You* (Tron Theatre / Birds of Paradise).

Alan McKendrick is a writer/director working across theatre, opera & film with organisations including the Arches, Untitled Projects, Tron, Traverse, NTS, GI, Riot Group, Bayerische Staatsoper München, Aldeburgh Music and Birmingham Contemporary Music Group. He also translates plays from German.

Linda McLean's latest play, *Sex and God*, was produced by Magnetic North in October 2012. *Any Given Day*, produced by Magic Theatre Company in San Francisco in 2012, won the Lella Rossy Playwrighting Award. *Fractures*, the French translation of *strangers, babies* opened in Lille on 25 January and transferred to Paris in March.

Joyce McMillan is theatre critic of *The Scotsman*, and also writes a political and social commentary column for the paper. She has been a freelance journalist, commentator and broadcaster based in Edinburgh for more than 25 years. Her book *The Traverse Theatre Story*, about the first twenty-five years of the Traverse, was published in 1988.

Alison Peebles, actor and director in theatre, film, TV and radio, recently worked with the National Theatre of Scotland on *My Shrinking Life* about living and working with Multiple Sclerosis. She is involved with research on the original staging of *Ane Satyre of the Thrie Estaites*, to be performed at Stirling Castle and Linlithgow Palace in June.

Gabriel Quigley studied an MA in English Literature and Theatre Studies at Glasgow University. Since 1995 she has acted extensively in theatre, radio and television and film. In 2006 she received a Herald Angel Award for her performance in the romantic comedy *Strawberries in January*. She lives in Glasgow.

Ben Wilkinson reviews new poetry for the *Guardian* and the *Times Literary Supplement*.

A pamphlet of poems, *The Sparks*, appeared in 2008; in 2010, he was shortlisted for the inaugural Picador Poetry Prize. He is working towards a first collection, *First Glance*.

Alex Williams is from Washington, DC. He has studied writing in Maine, US and Edinburgh, UK. He writes poetry, fiction, and criticism. He has worked as a barrista, a waiter, a pizza boy and a teacher. He currently works as a private investigator in San Francisco.

JL Williams' poetry has been published in journals including *Poetry Wales, The Wolf* and *Fulcrum*. Her first collection of poetry, *Condition of Fire*, was published in 2011 by Shearsman Books. She is Programme Manager at the Scottish Poetry Library. www.jlwilliamspoetry.co.uk

Fiona Wilson grew up in Aberdeen and now lives in New York City. Her work has appeared in *Poetry Review, New Writing Scotland, Literary Imagination, Northwords Now,* and elsewhere. She teaches at Sarah Lawrence College.

Ross Wilson was involved as a writer and actor in *The Happy Lands,* a feature film that premiered in 2013 to a sold out audience. His pamphlet collection, *The Heavy Bag,* was published by Calder Wood Press in November 2011.

David Yezzi's books of poems include *Azores* (2008) and *Birds of the Air* (2013). He is editor of *The Swallow Anthology of New American Poets* and executive editor of *The New Criterion*. He lives in New York City.

You can subscribe to *Edinburgh Review* at

http://www.edinburgh-review.com

Please join us on Facebook and Twitter.